The author of "Accused! Tahmari" has creatively brought to life the harm caused by hypocrisy as well as the wonderful triumph and possible outcomes of genuine love. Readers will be inspired to remember and embrace love as life's creative alternative to hypocrisy and hate.

REV. RONALD J. FOWLER
Pastor Laureate, Arlington Church of God,
Akron, Ohio

This book is a riveting account of the Bible story about the woman caught in adultery. I found it intriguing! Once I picked it up I could not put it down until I finished it. Lonnie did a fantastic job!

REV. KEVIN M. GOODE
Senior Pastor, The Church of the Harvest Church of God,
Middleburg Heights, Ohio

Other Books by
Lonnie-Sharon Williams

THE HEALINGS
*Three Stories of Miraculous
Healing from Scripture*

COMING HOME
Jakobi and Bartimaeus

ACCUSED!

Tahmari
The Woman Caught in Adultery

St. John 8:1-11

Lonnie-Sharon Williams

WESTBOW
PRESS®
A DIVISION OF THOMAS NELSON
& ZONDERVAN

WestBow Press books may be ordered through booksellers or by contacting:

WestBow Press
A Division of Thomas Nelson & Zondervan
1663 Liberty Drive
Bloomington, IN 47403
www.westbowpress.com
1 (866) 928-1240

ISBN: 978-1-5127-6265-5 (sc)
ISBN: 978-1-5127-6266-2 (e)

Print information available on the last page.

WestBow Press rev. date: 11/28/2016

ACKNOWLEDGEMENTS

I began this book some time ago and in a discussion with various Older Adult Sunday School classes, I was very surprised and impressed at how many of them (men and woman) voiced the opinion that the woman was "set-up." Why and how she was set up led to a heated discussion. One of my elderly students had me laughing, for when I explained that I was using their comments to write this story, she quipped, "She had no man who could lend a hand, and back in those days, a girl's gotta do what a girl's gotta do!"

You see, she and others felt this Jewish woman had to be desperate and at her last straw to go into this oldest profession and sympathized with her. But why was she desperate? Before the class was over, they were all on this Jewish prostitute's side although she broke one of God's commandments. Together we considered the life of this unnamed woman, giving her a name, a past, a present and a future.

Many things happened in the life of this woman before and while she became a prostitute. She had friends and enemies like any other person. What happened to her afterwards is not told in the Bible.

In that regard, I dedicate this book to the Older Adult Sunday Schools and Senior Vacation Bible classes held at The Church of the Harvest Church of God in Middleburg Heights (*formerly The Euclid Avenue Church of God)*, and the Church of God of Cleveland. There were many churches of various denominations and students too numerous to mention, but their study, comments, and insight into the scriptures gave new meaning to my fictional story.

I also thank the many pastors who have come alongside me to offer their encouragement, namely Reverend Kevin M. Goode, Reverend Abraham Jeter, Jr., Reverend James Roma, Pastor Laureate Reverend Dr. Ronald J. Fowler, Bishop Leanza Ford of True Faith Apostolic Bible Way Church, Minister Sarah Mack of Olive Grove Baptist Church, and the pastors and ministers of the Unity Pastors Fellowship of Cleveland.

Many thanks to the Township of Madison Library (Ohio), Mrs. Grace Reese and the Madison Ladies Book Club for using my books in their meetings, and to Caroline Peak, head director at the Collinwood Library. You have surely been a blessing.

Special thanks to my mentor, Pastor Joyce J. McIntyre of the Northeast Church of God (who also served as my proofreader), and my wonderful doctors and friends, the late Dr. Joseph Carter and Dr. Jessica R. Griggs at the MetroHealth Medical Centers in Cleveland, Ohio for her input on first century prostitutes. I salute everyone's continued encouragement and friendship.

CHARACTERS IN THIS STORY

Tahmari – Jewish prostitute
Aheelim – Man caught in situation with Tahmari
Abner – Livery and stable owner; Goshen's boss
Arbor – Eunuch - servant of Dorit
Batlan – Yelada's husband
Burlaht – Prostitute who died in childbirth
Dorit – Older prostitute and mentor
Elema – Goshen's baby sister
Eliah – Town official, friend to Teheran
Garner – Prostitute and friend of Tahmari
Goshen – Jepthun, a runaway slave
Halah – Josiah's wife
Jaffal and Jakri – Talkative twins
Josiah – Tahmari's uncle
Kiri – Prostitute and friend of Tahmari
Luchi – Prostitute and friend of Tahmari
Marka – Cousin Shallum's wife
Meka – Josiah's housekeeper
Mogdi – Tahmari's childhood friend
Najur – Arbor's friend and eunuch
Pashur – Abner's nephew and fellow worker
Pooka Family – Foreign merchant traders
Samtil – Town official

Shallum – Estranged Cousin of Josiah
Suri – Arbor's older sister
Teheran – Town official
Tirshah – Goshen's female friend; Abner's niece
Turza – Kiri's friend
Yelada – Young woman who was raped

* Scriptures are paraphrased from the New King James Version.

~1~

Lying on his sick bed, he turned his head to see his niece slip quietly into the room and begin fluffing the new straw pillows around his head. There was a soothing aromatic smell emanating from the pillow, which smelled like fresh-cut lavender, similar to the way she always smelled.

She was such a sweet and compassionate young girl and he could only smile as her hand smoothed his head and beard. Now his creased face showed more sadness than pain. His hair had begun to recede and his hair and beard had slowly gone from salt and pepper to steel gray. Once a robust man, he was now a thin replica of his old self.

Josiah thought back to when Tahmari first came to him less than 9 years ago. At that time, she was a small child and still in mourning for her parents, for their deaths were sudden and catastrophic. Her elderly grandparents were at a loss as to what they should do with her.

The child barely knew them for they lived far from their daughter and her husband and had only seen the child twice, once after her birth, and later on her third birthday. A few of her son-in-law's friends brought

Tahmari to them as they informed the older couple of their deaths.

After discussing the matter, it was agreed that she would go to her mother's older half-brother, Josiah, who had a frail wife. Josiah and his wife never had any children from their union. Halah was quiet and beautiful, but she was also barren. Although she had been somewhat sickly from her youth, Josiah loved her very much and at the betrothal promised her family he would always keep her safe and secure.

Because there were no children, the couple accepted the little girl with no argument and immediately fell in love with her for they now had a child. Not long after, both grandparents succumbed to pneumonia due to their old age.

When Josiah realized the little girl was very intelligent and learned quickly, he took the time to teach her to read, write and perform math skills, which she later found essential to helping with household accounting.

As his eyesight began to wane, he also thought it prudent for her to help him study the scrolls, yet most Jewish girls were never given that opportunity. He was a very religious man and instilled into her spiritual and moral values. In fact, he found she was more than an apt student and tutored her in Hebrew history and a few languages.

Josiah made sure Tahmari was careful with the scrolls

and encouraged her study. He loved her melodious voice and would sometimes allow her to read portions of scripture to him when his illness progressed and he could no longer do so.

While she was able, his wife Halah showed her how to use the loom, weave, and sew, as well as how to make beautiful jewelry using dyed cords and small stones. Her aunt's decorations on her head scarves included small beads and silver strips they collected from a silversmith friend in the city. The child loved creating special scarves for her aunt to wear to the synagogue for services. Many people complimented Halah on her beautiful scarves.

Halah was an excellent cook and bread maker and the two would make extra loaves to feed the poor as well as leave a loaf or two for the lepers on the hillside. They knew some of them would die without nourishment and the lepers found the bread very welcome.

Halah and Tahmari would discuss the words of the prophets and harmonize while singing the hymns that were taught at Temple, with her uncle sometimes joining in. In the evenings, prior to going to bed, together they would sing the songs of David while giving praise to Yahweh through their times of meditation.

Tahmari was an adept student and from her uncle learned how to whittle and make small flute-like instruments. She was friendly and had many friends her age, male and female.

As Tahmari grew a bit older, Josiah set up little wooden targets and showed her and a few of her friends how to throw small knives at the center. He taught her safety and to never use the small knife on anyone. Tahmari and he would play games together in the evenings and she never seemed to bore of his company, nor he hers. She was always obedient and never gave him any trouble.

Having experienced her parents' and aunt's deaths, the pain was nothing compared to her uncle's impending death. When his wife passed away, Tahmari mourned with him, but due to her aunt's illness they never had the same closeness she experienced with him.

Following Halah's passing, Josiah hired a woman to come a few days a week to help out. When Meka arrived, he could see her work was menial, for she was never really busy. He could see that was because Tahmari soon took it upon herself to do most of the cooking, cleaning and washing.

Josiah would sometimes chuckle to himself for he could see that Meka had become Tahmari's assistant. Still, he was grateful for her, for the older woman taught his niece things a mother would normally teach her daughter during her pre-teen years and the two developed a close relationship. When she started her menses, Meka was the one to explain many female facts to her.

As she began to mature, he realized she was a very pretty girl and knew it was about time for him to see about her betrothal to one of the nice young men in the village. Her large brown eyes were fringed with long lashes and her skin was smooth. Tahmari did not seem overly concerned about betrothal or marriage, yet she always had a small group of male friends around her, some of whom had begun to show interest prior to his illness. It was at this time he considered making a betrothal agreement with one of their parents.

The young man who he thought worthy of his niece was later promised to another for he had waited too long. Time had a way of getting away from him as well as the thought.

Now it was Josiah's time to die and his niece was taking his illness and latter days to heart. Although she called him "uncle," he knew Tahmari thought of him as "father".

~2~

Meka sat outside the door of Josiah's bedroom, allowing his niece to have some last moments with her dying uncle for she knew he would not last through the day. She was sad for the sake of the girl. The child had no relatives of whom she was aware, except a male cousin on her mother's side who seldom visited Josiah, even while her uncle was healthy.

Shallum was married and had a few children, but Josiah had neither expressed negative or any kind words toward him or his family. If they chanced to meet in the courtyard or the square, Josiah would acknowledge them with a nod. She doubted Josiah or Tahmari and the cousins had ever passed two words between them.

She thought of her own children, grandchildren, siblings, nieces and nephews and how they rallied around her when her husband passed away. Her house was full throughout Shiva, and on the Sabbath, following services at the Temple, the families would bring food to share, visit together, eating and talking until well in late afternoon or evening. Before they headed for their homes, there was always a lot of hugging and kissing.

Silently, she shook her head, knowing poor Tahmari would experience none of that.

Meka had encountered Shallum's shrew of a wife, Marka, in the marketplace, but no words were ever exchanged. She found Shallum's wife to be cold, calculating and a gossip. Even outside of the Temple, as everyone exited the courtyard, Shallum and his wife always walked side-by-side with their children silently following, not saying anything to anyone or to each other. After the services, all the other worshippers laughed and greeted each other warmly and walked in groups of families and friends.

Meka's heart went out to Tahmari. This poor child had no family or anyone to look after her – no one to weep with her. When Josiah passes away, what would the child do? She was approaching marriageable age but not betrothed, and there was no man to take her in or help her.

As she knelt beside her uncle's bed, Tahmari fought to hide her tears. Uncle Josiah tried to sit up a little as he gently and slowly rubbed her shiny brown hair which she had fixed into one long braid. He lifted her chin as he smiled at her.

"I know my dear," he rasped, "I know. I am so sorry you did not have brothers and sisters to be with you at this time. I will be going to a better place but you will be here all alone. There is a little money in the trunk beside my bed, which should tide you over for awhile. This house is not as nice as our old family home, but you will always have some place to live."

"I have found one thing and that is that Yahweh always sends someone or something to be with you. It may be budding flowers, or a small animal, but it may be an angel to watch over you. Just remember, I'll always look out for you," he promised.

Josiah wheezed, tried to sit up, but slowly slid into a weak semi-sitting position and again laid his hand on her head.

"I should have betrothed you last year to Mogdi, my friend's son, but my illness prevented it. I could tell he had feelings for you, yet no betrothal contract was ever made. At least that way, you would have had the promise of security with a good man and his family. I am so sorry, my dear. So very, very sorry. You deserve more than the best."

His hand continued to slowly stroke the top of her head.

"Your mother always loved this little house and would visit me when she was young. Your father was a good man and he made her happy. When you were born, Halah and I were as happy as your parents. It is too sad that your parents died so young and never saw you reach this age, for you have grown into a beautiful young lady."

Josiah gave a wheeze and a cough, swallowed and continued speaking in a low voice.

"When I am gone and you need money, think about selling this house. It is not a palace but it should bring a good price. It is not part of any inheritance that your cousin Shallum would be able to take from you as long as you are living here, so you can sell it with no problem. But if you die or move away, he would be your next living relative and the property will revert to him."

He gave another cough and wheeze and began sliding down, but he once again tried to sit up. He whispered a final warning to her.

"Beware of Shallum and his wife. They are too sneaky for my taste, but perhaps in the very near future you will find a nice young man to marry and have many children of your own. You have a compassionate nature and have been more than a daughter to me and Halah. I give praise every day to Yahweh, for you have been the daughter we never had. You've been such a blessing."

Slowly he removed his hand from her hair and as he coughed, she could hear the death rattle in his chest. Giving her one last smile, he slowly lay back down on his pillow and closed his eyes.

"Remember, my dear," he whispered, "I will always love you – in life and in death my love will always be with you."

Wheezing softly for a few seconds, the room soon became silent.

When Tahmari raised her head, she knew her uncle had drawn his last breath. He had turned his head slightly away from her. His eyes were set and looked toward the ceiling.

~3~

Hearing no further conversation, Meka silently entered the room, put her arms around her charge and walked her to the front of the house. Returning toward Josiah's bed, she took her left hand and slowly closed Josiah's eyes — with her right hand she pulled the coverlet over his lifeless body. He had such a sweet smile on his face as she covered his head.

"My family and I will inform the townspeople of his death and help you prepare his body for burial," she said quietly. "Go and lie down, child, and get some rest, for we will soon be very busy with Josiah's preparations."

Tahmari nodded, acknowledging she knew they must begin the purchase of burial oils, laying out his burial clothes and the hiring of mourners.

Looking out the door, she saw a small dog with his nose to the ground, snuffling around as if he was searching for something. She smiled at the little dog for she could see he was a bit older than a puppy. Noticing her presence, he looked up and stared at her. Again, putting his nose to the ground, he trotted around the corner of the house and disappeared from her sight.

She knew Uncle Josiah was dying, for the doctors had told her about six or seven months ago that he would probably last only two to three months. But he was stronger than everyone thought. He had repeatedly told her that Yahweh's time was not the same as human time and what did the doctors know? She knew her uncle had been trying to prolong his life so that she would not be left alone.

One thing about death, she thought: death always has a way of catching up with the body.

Josiah's Shiva and burial were well-attended services. Shiva itself was very crowded. Tahmari knew he had a lot of friends and acquaintances, and most came to pay their respects, many of whom she had never before seen. Families arrived, and many of the women came with bowls and plates of food for the after-burial meal, bringing their specialties and other dishes that would last for some time so that Tahmari would not have to fix food afterwards. Some left coins, mourning veils, and soaps, oils, and perfumes for her.

Jewish tradition teaches that sitting 'Shiva' was healthy and healing for the bereaved and it was so for Tahmari. She was pleased with the condolences and gifts which were given and the many stories shared by friends of Uncle Josiah, who told many kind tales of him from his youth. Shiva generally lasted six to seven days after the burial, but many of her uncle's friends came for more than 10 days, for which she was very pleased.

Shiva does not occur on the Sabbath, so for a few days she was alone, yet the priests who were her uncle's friends, came after sundown for an half-hour and repeated prayers with her.

Men who came in long robes sat and read aloud from one of her uncle's scrolls. Tahmari only brought out two scrolls for she was afraid one of the men would ask for them and she did not want to give them away. They were very cordial and did not ask.

There was one older man, however, who fingered one of the scrolls reverently and smiled at her. She was not sure if he knew she could read them or not, so she just quietly returned his smile. She could only think of the scrolls as a part of her legacy from her uncle.

Conversation ensued where many told of favors Josiah had performed for them, and how he would give money and food to those who had none. One woman said she had no mourning clothes to wear following her husband's death. Josiah's wife, Halah, had passed away some time before, so he gave her a few pretty robes for mourning and to wear to Temple. When she remarried, she looked beautiful in one of Halah's gowns. Many women, young and old, hugged Tahmari as they gave their condolences before leaving her house.

Tahmari was now alone. Her uncle's friends no longer

visited and her childhood friends no longer came around. She had no one to talk to and her friend, Meka, would soon be leaving her.

◆

Josiah's ailments started with a slight cough a few years back, and Josiah began doctoring himself as if he had a cold, but over time his coughing spells became worse, sometimes spitting blood. He tried his best to keep his illness quiet, but the girl was very astute.

As each of her friends announced their betrothals and they were later invited to the wedding celebrations, Josiah began to realize his time and his money was getting short. Too much money had been spent on his illness. Who would take care of his beloved niece once he passed away?

He had looked over the young men in the area, but he had waited too long. There was a man by the name of Samtil who had approached him, but he wanted someone a bit closer to her age. Josiah knew Samtil was not very old but he wanted a younger man for his niece. He felt Samtil was probably looking for a younger woman to marry to give him healthy children. He was of a nice build and cordial, one of the town's officials and quite well-to-do. However, Josiah wanted to wait a few more years before he considered an older man

But such was not to be the case. Time passed and he never informed Tahmari of the man's offer for her.

Although she had a little money saved, it was quickly depleting. Her food supply was low. Meka had purchased a few items for her larder, but her youngest daughter had recently married and would soon move to another area with her new husband. Meka, was now packing to move with her daughter and new son-in-law.

Soon Tahmari would be completely alone.

~4~

Months passed and the loneliness was unbearable. As the money began to dwindle, Tahmari had earlier explained to her friend, Meka, she would have to find another position, for she would soon be unable to pay her for her services. However, Meka had told her to not worry about it. Her friend refused to find another position, saying she would continue staying with her charge without payment.

Unbeknownst to her uncle, Tahmari had begun selling some of the more beautiful pieces of jewelry given to her by her parents before their deaths and a few from her uncle. She still had a few other pieces from her mother and the grandmother she barely knew, as well as the jewelry pieces she made with Aunt Halah. Tahmari had even begun making bracelets and small jewelry pieces which a few of the merchants would purchase. It was not a lot of money, but gave her extra funds for food, candles, and oil.

She still had a few of her uncle's friends asking her to make bracelets, hair pins and ornaments for their daughters and they would always pay her for her work. Her goal was to become a jewelry maker and be able to sell her pieces in the marketplace. She loved looking at the traders' wares whenever she went into town, some of which gave her ideas for her own jewelry.

Within a few years of her arrival, her uncle's frail wife became very ill and passed away. He was soon a widower and he and his late wife never had any children. He received many items from Tahmari's maternal grandmother, and was pleased to give her those and the many items of jewelry he had purchased for his wife. She also had a few pieces Halah inherited from her family as well as their wedding presents.

When she was about 10 or 11 years of age, he gave her the most beautiful silver bracelet. It was encircled with beautiful rich stones and she knew it was costly. Tahmari treasured the bracelet because it made her feel very rich and close to her uncle.

~5~

She was receiving many unfavorable looks from the beggars in the section where she sat. Tahmari shifted in her small seating area and pulled her knitting skeins closer to her side. She heard the men's loud mumbling and griping, but chose to ignore their words. What else could she do except beg alms outside the Temple? She found it was useless to try to sell her knitted items or the few jewelry pieces she had made, for everyone passed her by without looking at her wares.

She could see some of the infirmed whispering in a group about her, but she was desperately in need of money. True, she could see those men had physical infirmities and tried to ignore their whispers.

It wasn't as if she had not observed that some of the men would walk past, and either winked or smiled at her and, out of habit, she smiled in return, for any amount of money they dropped into her cup was acceptable. She was at the point of accepting whatever monies she could receive.

Eventually, one of the men who had been whispering,

came toward her. She could see one of his legs was shorter than the other and he was leaning heavily on his crutch.

He leaned toward her and grumpily said if she was "really" infirmed, she was begging in the wrong area.

"Females do not beg alms in this area by the Temple. You should go somewhere else and beg because people, mainly men, are ignoring the true needy beggars and more likely heading toward you to drop their coins, instead of coming toward us."

Tahmari was already self-conscious, but now she became more so. What else could she do?

She saw a slight movement behind the man and observed two Temple guards and some doorkeepers heading in her direction. Behind them trotted the same small dog she remembered a few years back from the day her uncle passed. Tahmari observed that one of the doorkeepers was trying to shoo the dog away. She did not know much about dogs or their ages but figured he was perhaps around two or three years of age. She could see he was not afraid of the man but obediently left the area. Perhaps this was not the first time he'd been shooed by a doorkeeper, she thought.

Comprehension set in. Oh no! Someone must have reported her. She did not want to make a scene, yet she was as needy as anyone. The lead guard was stern of face, but his eyes were not grim. The head doorkeeper was not old, yet not young either. Their uniforms and robes were spotless. All had beautifully woven yarmulkes on their heads with colors denoting their ranks, and all carried small swords at their sides. She did not believe the guards would use their weapons, although she could see the situation would not bode well for her.

Embarrassed and a bit queasy from lack of food, she put her head down in dismay. The head guard stopped beside her as he stooped near her, bending his body toward where she was sitting, and quietly informed her of her mistake.

"I am sorry to tell you this, young lady, but you cannot beg alms here. This area is not for females, but for infirmed males. We can see you are not ill, infirmed or afflicted. If you were disabled in any way, I would direct you to the area for females. You will probably receive a few alms here, but only from men for the wrong reasons and this is not allowed in the areas near the Temple. I am so sorry, my dear."

He had placed one hand under her elbow as he spoke, helping her to stand, waited while she picked up her skin of water and knitting materials, then led her away from the beggars' area. She watched as the other guards and the doorkeepers returned to their normal positions around the Temple.

Speaking close to her hear, he whispered, "You don't know me, but I knew you when you were a small child. Tahmari, isn't it? I had just become a young Temple guard when I met your Uncle Josiah. He had taken it upon himself to help some women who were in the wrong occupation. With his help, they were able to have their case heard before a magistrate and received favorable judgment. A wonderful man he was. I was saddened to hear of his passing."

"I understand your plight, but there is nothing I can do to help you. You're a very pretty girl, so perhaps Yahweh will bless you with a young man who will be able to offer you some type of security through marriage. This most certainly is not the place for you."

Tahmari nodded her head in understanding and followed the guard to another side of the area. Glancing at the few coins in her cup she gave a slight smile for there was no doubt the guard was correct, as well as the grumpy man with the crutch. All of the coins she received were given to her from men who came toward her as they searched her face and figure prior to dropping the coins in her cup. She did not wear a covering for her face so they could see she was not a prostitute, and they could tell she was not married for a husband would not allow her to be in this area.

As she and the guard moved around the corner, he placed a few more coins in her cup, patted her arm and left her.

~6~

It was then she noticed a pretty young woman watching her. She had on a lot of makeup, especially on her eyes and lips, and gave a slight smile at her. The woman carried a vessel for water on her left hip and a long bag on her shoulder as she headed toward the town well. Tahmari kept walking, putting her head down as she kept her eyes to the ground.

She took the coins from her cup and placed them in her script bag, folded it into her girdle for safekeeping, and headed to the other side of the well. Using the edge of her robe, she wiped the cup clean. There was water in a large gourd on the small shelf to the side of the well, for which she was thankful. First she filled her cup with water from the gourd, then refilled her water skein which she carried with her. She slowly sipped from the cup while watching the woman out of the corner of her eye. The young woman quietly approached and began to draw water for her own vessel.

The small dog, which seemed to always be near, stared at her with his large brown eyes. She leaned down and patted his head. Believing him to be thirsty also, she scratched a hole into the dirt and poured water into it. She was surprised the hole did not become muddy once she added the water, but stayed clear. The dog's eyes looked at her with thanks and began lapping up the water. When it was low, she poured more water into the small pool until he seemed satisfied.

It was past the time for procuring water from the well, but believed this woman drew water at this time on a daily basis and understood this was the time those who were pagan generally came to the well.

Tahmari noticed the woman was at least five or six years older than herself, but wore somewhat nice clothing and a beautiful scarf. Although pretty, she had wide hips and reeked of heavy perfume. Instantly Tahmari realized the young woman was one of the village prostitutes.

She didn't know much about such women, but the type of scarf gave her away. It was the type that could be shifted to her face and used as a veil. She knew there were quite a few in and around the town. As far as she knew, her uncle never utilized their services, yet remembered he did have two or three prostitutes who would at times come around to visit him and a few would bring delicacies they had made and even brought them barley soup.

On one of the visits by a few older prostitutes, one of the women told her that Uncle Josiah had defended them and they would never forget what he had done. She asked her uncle what did they mean, but he would wave her questions aside and smile.

Tahmari never again asked how he defended them, but believed they still appreciated his help for he enjoyed their company.

When he passed away, a few prostitutes came to the house, bringing food, and offering their condolences. After the last of the mourners left the house, she found a small bag with coins inside and a small pot of stew beside the brazier. Since they were the only ones who visited late in the evening, she realized it was the two prostitutes who left the money and the stew, for which she was very grateful.

~7~

"Good day," the woman began while looking directly into Tahmari's face and lifted one eyebrow. "I saw you trying to beg alms awhile ago, and then saw the Temple doorkeepers remove you. Are your ill, or do you just need money?"

At first Tahmari kept her head down and did not speak for she felt the woman was a bit forward in asking personal questions. When she realized the woman was innocently questioning, she decided to respond.

"I am not ill or infirmed, as you can see—just in need of money. The money my uncle left for me is almost depleted. I didn't know what else to do. In a few days I will begin to starve for I have very little money and no man to care for me so I decided to beg alms. I don't know how else to raise money and now I know that it was not right for me to beg."

Embarrassed, she lowered her head for fear the tears in her eyes would flow down her cheeks.

"The people call me Kiri," the woman quietly informed her, "and I can sympathize with your situation. I can't help you, but perhaps a friend of mine will be able to do so. There is a woman in town by the name of Dorit. She and her servant, Arbor, live in a small house heading toward the river. She might be able to help you for she helped me when I was down and out."

"You'll like her and her manservant, who was once a servant for one of Jerusalem's officials who passed away. Arbor, that's his name, has been a servant to Dorit for many years. He was ill and dying when Dorit found him on the streets, took him in and nursed him back to health and he's been in this town and with her ever since. Come with me and I'll take you to her."

They walked a little way and Kiri placed her water pot near the door of a small house. She leaned over and covered the top of the vessel to keep flying bugs from settling inside, and then they both continued on. Behind them trotted the little brown dog which seemed to suddenly appear out of nowhere. At first she thought the dog belonged to the woman, but when Kiri did not acknowledge its presence, she believed he just may be a stray.

Tahmari felt a bit uneasy, but the woman seemed harmless enough. She had her small knife in her girdle, and placed her hand on the handle just in case it was needed. She then took the time to look around in the event she needed to run away, but could see the woman posed no real danger.

Tahmari's stomach began to growl and she knew it

was loud enough for Kiri to hear. They came to a halt and when Kiri sat down on one of the boulders, she also sat. Kiri reached into the long bag on her shoulder, pulled out a smaller bag and handed it to her. Loosening the drawstring, Tahmari looked inside the bag and saw a nice portion of smoked fish, a few small chunks of cheese, some raisins and dates, and a few pieces of unleavened bread.

"You look as if you could use this food more than I could," Kiri said as she smiled. "Don't worry about me, I have more at home. I always carry a small lunch for whenever I leave home, but I've already eaten and this is what is left over. Go ahead, eat it."

The two women settled themselves on a large boulder as Tahmari took the bag and began to chew. It had been some time since she ate a decent meal and she let her eyes thank Kiri as she stuffed the food into her mouth. Once her hunger was sated, she began to explain her situation.

Hearing a slight whimpering, Tahmari looked down and there was the little dog. He had moved closer but sat on his haunches a safe distance behind the women and began whimpering a bit louder. Separating a piece of bread and meat, she fed it to the little dog.

"My name is Tahmari and I live on the north side of town. You don't know how much I appreciate the food. I didn't use all of it, so there's some left for you to eat later."

She pulled the drawstring tight and was about to

return the small bag, but the woman waved her hand. "Don't worry about me. I'm all right. Besides I haven't missed any meals lately and it looks like I need to miss a few anyway." She patted her hips and gave a small chuckle as she did so.

"Do you mind if I feed a little more to the dog? He looks as if he is hungry also."

"Sure, go ahead. It would probably spoil and I'll have to throw it away."

Bending down, Tahmari gave the dog bits and pieces of food. He trotted over to the water, lapped some more, and once again sat back on his haunches. The two women laughed.

"I believe he's thanking us," Kiri chuckled. "Let's go visit my friend." Eventually, the two continued walking.

~8~

They soon reached a small neat house on the edge of town and saw a dark-skinned middle-aged man sitting on a stool beside the door. He had beautiful brown eyes, long dark lashes and a small beard, unlike those worn by the men of the area. Seeing them heading his way, he stood and Tahmari could see he was tall and regal. He wore a long dark robe and a small knitted skullcap, similar to the Jewish yarmulke, which partially covered his head of braids which reached below his shoulders.

"Good morning, Kiri." With a slight bow, he greeted the prostitute in a slightly-accented voice although his Aramaic was impeccable. "It is always good to see a friend of Dorit. She enjoys visitors and they have been scarce lately."

"It is also good to see you, Arbor. You are looking quite well. Is Dorit available right now to see us? I brought a friend and her name is Tahmari, from the other side of town."

The man's eyes searched Tahmari's face as if he was trying to recognize her, then smiled as he slowly turned, indicating they should follow him into the house. Perhaps it was his brown face, but she believed he had the whitest teeth she had ever seen and his smile was welcoming.

The house was very warm, and seated in a low chair covered with a sheep-skinned coverlet was a small woman. The weather was balmy and she noticed a bit of perspiration on the woman's face. Tahmari could see she was ill, but she had a bright smile on her face.

Her sallow skin and breasts sagged from loss of weight and there was a strange smell about her. She also had on a lot of makeup and while her cheeks were thin and flushed, she believed the woman had been very pretty in her youth.

"Please make yourself at home, my dears," she began as she waved one hand around the area of the room. "I'm sorry I cannot get up to properly greet you, but you're always welcome here. What have you been up to lately, Kiri? Is all well with you?"

Kiri bent over and kissed the top of the woman's head, then pulled up two stools from beside a small table so they could sit in front of the older woman."

"All is well, my love. Dorit, this is my new friend, Tahmari. We met at the well."

The older woman's eyes were very bright and having taken care of her uncle, Tahmari realized the older woman was somewhat feverish. As they sat before her, it wasn't long before she saw that Dorit had begun to perspire heavily and she was slowly becoming weaker.

"Arbor," she smiled at him, "is it possible we might have a few honey cakes left? He's a marvelous cook and he knows I love honey cakes, so you'll have to try at least one or two. Also, please fix a few cups of unfermented wine to help the cakes go down. You girls will stay for a short repast, won't you?"

Kiri gave a quick nod, which settled the question.

It seemed Arbor had either read his mistress' mind or was used to receiving this instruction from his mistress, for he immediately put before them a plate of honey cakes and a tray with three small cups. He bowed and discreetly left them to return to his seat in front of the door.

During their visit, two more women arrived and Arbor escorted them to his mistress, went to the rear of the house and produced two more stools. Within minutes he brought more wine and honey cakes. The arrivals also wore heavy makeup and perfume and were about the same age as Kiri. They were introduced to Tahmari by Kiri as Garner and Luchi, and a pleasant visit continued.

The honey cakes were delicious and were eaten as they discussed the weather and various fashions they had observed from the merchants in the square. Kiri showed Dorit an expensive scarf that one of her male friends had given her as a present.

It was not long before Dorit's eyes began to slowly close and then flicker open, only to close again. It was apparent to them she was fighting to stay awake. Tahmari could see she enjoyed company and to have four women in front of her was a blessing. Eventually, she could not fight sleep for it soon overtook her and the older woman began to quietly snore.

Almost on cue, Arbor silently returned to the room and proceeded to pull the coverlet across her chest a little tighter as he turned and looked at the four women. As if on signal, they all stood and began heading toward the door. As Tahmari was the last to pass by, he took her hand and folded her fingers over the coins he had placed on her palm and put his fingers over his lips to express a hush. She smiled her thanks and the man smiled back.

"Thank you for visiting, ladies; I know she's happiest when you come. She will be resting for some time now." Arbor gave a slight bow, following them out as he returned to his seat outside the door after patting each woman on the shoulder.

~9~

They walked a little distance before anyone spoke. Tahmari finally asked, "Dorit is very ill, isn't she? I believe she is feverish."

"Yes," said Kiri softly and the others nodded. "She has a violent illness and tends to be in pain, but Arbor fixes her a concoction using special herbs and leaves that deadens the pain somewhat and gives her rest. It started in her stomach and traveled to her hips. We've never seen them, but we've been told she has strange boils and bumps on her arms, legs and thighs. It is an infectious disease that prostitutes sometimes suffer after getting it from a client, and she's had it for over two years. She sometimes has drainage, but Arbor keeps her clean and takes very good care of her."

The women continued walking as they discussed Dorit's manservant, Arbor.

"There is nothing about medicine that Arbor does not know. In fact, he's a better healer than most doctors in this area. Arbor does not talk much about his previous life, or about what he does while Dorit sleeps. Dorit once told us there are some things one must keep secret, so we keep our thoughts to ourselves. Arbor keeps his own secrets and he sees things many of us do not see for he is very observant."

"In the beginning, when she first noticed something was wrong with her body, she called for the doctors, to no avail. Arbor then put her in his small cart, and took her to a doctor who the townspeople say is a well-known "healer", but he refused to treat her when he saw her discharge. The man didn't say anything to Dorit, but when he looked at Arbor, he shook his head. That's when he knew it was very bad."

"The healer said the illness she has is caused by her occupation and told him she would die within a few months. He did what he could, but Arbor refused to give up on Dorit and began doctoring her himself. We don't know where he learned his medicine, but he's good. She has been fine for over two years through Arbor's care, but we all can see she's nearing death."

"We've even had some of our clients ask for him to come to their homes when their families or servants become ill and their doctors have given up hope. His care for Dorit has lasted over two years, but she's failing now. Arbor has never lost a patient under his care and he is trying to keep Dorit alive as long as possible. He once said if her pain becomes unbearable, then he will make sure she goes peacefully."

"We try to visit with Dorit as much as possible for we

can see she's weakening and does not have very long to live. She enjoys having her friends visit. Even some of her clients come to sit and talk with her, for Dorit is a great listener."

"We don't know what will become of Arbor when Dorit dies, but he's resourceful and Dorit has been paying him so he will have some income in the event he decides to move on. He has a few friends who visit him and a woman who comes to visit him every once in awhile. We're not sure who she is, but she's very well-to-do for she comes in a nice cart filled with fruits and nuts for him and for Dorit, along with a few servants."

"For a long time, we thought she was friend to Dorit, but Dorit only says the woman knew Arbor from 'way back,' whatever that means. As far as we know, he has no family."

One of the two other women looked at the sky and then at Kiri, who nodded her head in response.

"We have to leave you now, but you are welcome to visit Dorit whenever you wish. I presume you realize by now what we do for a living. We live our lives in sin, but many of us believe in the wise God who is our Father as well as any Jewish citizen of this town. Dorit taught us about the unseen God, praying, and giving tithes to the Temple and we do so in accordance with the laws of Moses. We pay our taxes to Caesar, and we say our prayers although we are not allowed inside the Temple.

Many of us were raised believing in other gods, but now some of us don't."

"You should know that no matter where you are, you can always count on us and on Dorit and Arbor, even if you just want someone to talk to."

After saying their goodbyes, the three women turned and headed in the same direction, while Tahmari continued toward her home. She planned to visit with Dorit again.

~10~

Tahmari made a point of visiting Dorit at least once every few days. Dorit was a good listener and she found herself pouring out her woes. She told her about Uncle Josiah and how good he was to her. After a few months, she brought up the idea of becoming one of the harlots. She had met with Kiri and other prostitutes and they gave her information on their lifestyles. They told her there were very few Jewish prostitutes, but those women tended to keep to themselves.

Dorit and Arbor said if it was money she needed, they would help her, but she refused to take any more from them, saying she wanted to be able to have an income of her own.

Whenever she would visit Dorit, the two would discuss Jewish history, sometimes singing many of the songs she once sang with her uncle and aunt, but stopped accepting money from them.

She was not sure if Arbor was paying her for her time with Dorit or because he could see she was very poor. She did not want the manservant to believe she came only for money.

She came because she enjoyed their company.

◆

Finally, the time came when she realized she was completely destitute. Having no funds and very little food, it was not long before she hesitantly approached Dorit with the idea of becoming a prostitute.

In the beginning, Dorit would not discuss it with her. She would suddenly nod into sleep, but Tahmari knew she did not want to talk to her about it. After a while, the older woman decided to explain the life of a prostitute, warning her it was not a good profession.

"You've spoken with the other ladies and know the hardships. We call our work the 'desperate profession'. Although many women choose to become one for various reasons, I do not recommend that they do."

"You're too nice a girl to get mixed up in this. You will have few positives and many, many negatives by becoming one. First, you're very young and still a virgin. Secondly, there are downsides when you consider various diseases that can be passed on to you by men who are not clean. Third, and most importantly, you are Jewish. My dear, Tahmari, a gently raised Jewish girl should never think about becoming a harlot."

"But there are Jewish prostitutes, Dorit."

"Yes, but they don't let their customers know. There are men who are devious and will try to cheat you, then there are those who have unusual lusts. Just because a man looks prosperous does not mean he is disease free or has strange sexual desires. There is also the problem where you could become pregnant — and which man would you believe to be the father of your baby? You would not be able to prove it, even if you were sure."

"There are very few positives in this business and the women are only in it because they feel they will be able to make money and be independent—not a lot of money, mind you, but enough to take care of themselves. There are men, Jewish and pagan, who will abuse you, and I would hate to have that happen to you."

"I do not want you to starve so I would like to give you another option. You can move here and live with me and Arbor. We're good company and you would not have to worry about starving. You're a beautiful girl and may find a good Jewish man who could give you protection."

Tahmari smiled and shook her head 'no'. "I have a home of my own, but I do appreciate your offer."

"I know you want to stay in your own home, but please, child," Dorit leaned over and patted her shoulder, "do go home and think over what I just said. I know you're one of Abraham's children, so please pray over it then come back to me with your reply. Remember, you are always welcome here."

Dorit turned her head toward Arbor, who stood

nearby. As they locked eyes, both nodded then the older woman turned back to Tahmari.

"I will pray that Yahweh will take care of you and give you an answer to your request."

Slowly Dorit's eyes began to close as Arbor walked Tahmari to the door, patting her shoulder while his other hand surreptitiously placed a few coins into her palm. She put her hand over his and returned the pat and coins as she exited from the house.

~11~

Arbor fanned Dorit's face, and with one hand behind her head, laid her lightly on the pallet he had made for her near the vicinity of the cooking area. The older woman smiled gratefully at her devoted servant and slowly closed her eyes from the pain.

"I want you to do as I ask, Arbor. No shirking this time. It would be much better for her if you do. Neither I nor you want this but she has made her decision and it was not up to us, but she's old enough to know her own mind. This life is hard enough as it is, but I don't want her first experience to be worse than what it will be."

The eunuch said nothing, but nodded his head in understanding. He looked closely at Tahmari as she looked askance at him. He knew without a doubt it would be best for her if he carried out his mistress's wishes. She was so pretty and young. He settled his face while lowering his lashes, for she could see he was trying to avoid looking at her.

Life was not fair to women, whether Jewish or pagan, he thought. The day will come when things will change for women, but sadly not now. It is too sad the poor girl has reached this point in her life. She should be cooking for a husband and a few little ones, not having him prepare her for a life of sin. Although he had no personal god, what she wanted was not good for her upbringing and faith.

With his head bent, slowly he continued to bathe Dorit's face from perspiration. After a moment or two he stood and shook himself.

Dorit could see his thoughts as he began washing his hands and then motioned for the young woman to follow him behind the curtain which led into a back room.

"Don't worry, Arbor. I understand," Tahmari whispered behind him. "I'm not a child you know. My friend, Meka, explained a woman's body and the sex act to me when I was young."

Dorit eyes followed from her pallet as Tahmari walked behind the calm stately man toward the back of the house.

For the first 15 or so minutes, very little noise was heard from the back, except the eunuch's low tones as he gave instructions and then the woman's soft response.

Soon a sharp cry came from the back.

Dorit glanced up once again and watched as Arbor came toward the table, retrieved a few pieces of cloth and a bowl of warm water near the brazier. He looked sorrowfully at her before returning to the back room.

It wasn't long before the servant returned to his mistress' side, bent down and whispered, "It is done, as you requested. She'll be okay in a few minutes. She's cleaning herself and will be out soon."

"Good," she whispered. "I know this is hard on you, Arbor, but for her own sake it must be done, otherwise her first time will be horrible."

Giving a gentle sigh, she closed her eyes. "I am so tired. I'm going to take a short nap and will be up in a few minutes."

They both knew her 'few minutes' would be at least a few hours, but neither said anything further.

Arbor slowly washed his hands and headed toward the cooking area. He pulled a large bowl toward himself and began to shell peas to add to the previously cut-up vegetables and lentils in preparation for a stew for the three of them.

A few minutes later Tahmari joined them as she slowly walked from behind the curtain, noticing Dorit was snoring softly on her pallet with a slightly crooked smile on her face.

"She's not well, is she Arbor?"

"No, but she's doing much better today. I believe it is because you are here. Whenever she has visitors, I notice she fares much better. I don't know if this is because visitors keep her from dwelling on her pain or if she has conversation with someone other than myself. She tends to try to hide how she actually feels." Arbor gave a slight smile.

Tahmari sat on a short stool near the eunuch and

watched as he added more ingredients to the stew. Everything was beginning to smell marvelous and she could hear her stomach growling in anticipation.

"I know you wish to know more about Dorit and myself so she has given me permission to tell you about our lives."

He stirred the pot of stew and added a few spices to the broth and then stirred again as the aroma wafted throughout the small house. Speaking in a soft tone, he stood in the middle of the room and recounted his life.

~12~

"My master purchased me in an Ethiopian city from the traders who took my family there. I was not born an eunuch, but was made one at an early age when our village was raided. The traders sold me very cheaply for they did not believe eunuchs were worth much money, but they knew I was young and well built. My new master purchased me and was surprised to learn that I had already lost my manhood at such a young age. He tried in vain to acquire my parents who had also been made slaves. The family who purchased them would not sell them and I tend to believe they were not ill treated."

"My older sister, Suri, and I were sold to my master as children. Suri was sickly, became very ill and later died. I never really got to know her, so we were never very close. I did, however, tend to miss her when I was young because she was my only family and a part of me, as well as my homeland."

"My master and his other slaves and servants trained me to be the type of servant that would be useful to him. I was young when he purchased me and unlike others in my situation, I believe he loved me as if I was his son, for he had no children."

Arbor moved the pot from one side of the brazier to the other, where the heat was not so intense.

"My master was older and very wealthy. He had many slaves and servants who helped raise me, took me under their wings, taught me how to cook, clean and do everything for him. I was also taught how to sew, select materials, weave, and work the loom. I am trained in the use of dyes, including the use of herbs and medicines, and how to run a household. He had special clothes made for me and I would drive his wagon to various places when he had to conduct business. I happily use those skills now. I was with him more than 25 years."

"When my master passed away, his nephew and heir took control and since he had no need for extra servants, he put me and a few others out of the house. He released me, so I was free, but not able to live outside of my master's house. I believe most of the others were able to find employment for they were not slaves. I have found many men do not really want an adult eunuch around unless they have need of one. I could have served as a valet, but I believe there is a stigma attached to an 'unmanly man' as well as my skin color. I had no means of taking care of myself. For although I acted as a free man, I was still a slave."

"Slaves are not given wages so I was unable to purchase

food and other necessary items. I slept beside the buildings near the Temple and tried to beg alms, but many Jews are prejudiced against my darker skin. I would go behind the inns at night and dig in the waste that was thrown out. Sometimes I would eat food items with worms on them. There were times I slept in the open, against a building or under a wagon. There was once a very nice woman who gave me a blanket when it was cold, but one night while I slept, another homeless person stole it from me. I was too weak to fight him for it and after stabbing me in the side, he quickly ran away with it. I almost starved to death and had gone down to nothing but skin and bones."

He paused and frowned as if remembering this horrible period of time.

"From lack of nourishment, I had become dizzy and fell in an alley, cracking my head. Dorit happened to come upon me and soon requested a few men to pick me up and carry me to her house. She washed and bandaged the cut on my head and had taken off my ragged clothes to bathe me. When I awakened, she had swaddled my body and that was when she realized I was an eunuch, but she continued to nurse me back to health."

"Within a few weeks time, I had gained weight and my hair and beard were neatly trimmed. The stab wound healed and you can hardly see the scar my head experienced when I blacked out."

"To this day, Dorit has never once asked me any

questions as to how I came to be in the state she found me and it was weeks before I finally told her my situation. I felt I owed her that much because I could not pay her for saving my life."

"She didn't care, and told me I could live with her until I was ready to leave and when that time came, she would not stop me, but hoped I would remain with her. So I remained and have never regretted it. In fact, there are those in the area who believe that Dorit purchased me from my past owner. I have no papers to show otherwise and no one questions her."

~13~

"It was some time before I realized what she did for a living or how she always had money, especially since she had no man in the house. I was also amazed that she owned her own home for she was not a widow. Food was always available and she had many male visitors, whom I later realized were many of her customers. When she would put her veil on her head prior to men coming, I soon realized what she did for a living."

He turned and scanned her face. "I'm quite sure she would have told me herself, for I was not uninformed of the ways of women who have no men to care for them. To this day, she has not actually told me. I believe it's because she felt I already knew."

He put his head down for a few seconds, soon lifting it to continue.

"Dorit's illness stems from a disease passed on to her by an infected man. She knew who gave it to her and told me. This man never acknowledged this disease to her for it is a horrible disease. I believe he knew, yet he kept frequenting Dorit. Once they were having relations and she noticed something about his lower body. When she finally asked, he laughed it off, yet he was suffering from it. By then she had contracted his disease, for he'd given it to her. That's when she stopped having men come to her. Yet, she still has customers who are her friends. They still come around, but now only to visit or tell her their problems, for she is a good listener."

"Dorit's best friend also had relations with that man. She had no one to care for her and she died last year from the same disease. The disease spreads throughout the body over time and we were not sure how long she had contracted it, but I believe she had it long before Dorit. We tried to get her friend to come live with us, but she refused. She continued to offer sacrifices to appease her god, believing this was the way her god was punishing her."

He stopped again and looked as if he wanted to cry.

"This disease is unto death. When she finally told me the man's name, I made sure that man would never bother her again or touch any of the others. To this day, Dorit does not know how he died. She believes he must have succumbed to the disease. He had a wife, whom he abused constantly. There were children—I believe two boys. At least he had stopped having sexual relations with his wife early on; more than likely prior to contracting the disease, for which I am quite sure she was happy."

Looking Tahmari straight into her eyes, he quietly

emphasized, "That man will never give that disease to another woman. I made sure of that!"

Tahmari realized what he was saying and schooled her face so she would not show shock or surprise.

Sighing, Arbor continued. "When the Roman soldiers found his body on the outskirts of the Jerusalem hillside, no questions were ever asked by his wife or the authorities. Once the soldiers saw the bumps and boils on what was left of his sexual organs, they knew what it was. In fact, those soldiers did not bring the body to town to his wife for they knew who he was, but had her come to identify it. He was a well-known man to the Temple and a city official. That good woman did not give him a true burial and in my opinion, he didn't deserve one. He must have contracted the disease from prostitutes in another area because none of the women here caught it."

"I understand he was quite well-to-do with servants, property and animals. He had married a younger woman to produce an heir, which she did."

"Personally and in my opinion, she's better off without him. I believe she's happy he's gone and has now gone on with her life. She is still young and nice looking, especially so since he is no longer with her. With her inheritance she will probably marry again and will attract someone who can give her the love she should have received from her husband."

"She comes to visit with me every once in a while. I

don't know exactly if she knew how her husband died, but one time when she visited me, she handed me a small pouch that contained quite a bit of money. All she said was, 'thank you, Arbor'. She comes to see me on the occasions she visits with friends in town."

Arbor walked toward the brazier, stirred the pot and sat on another chair near Tahmari.

~14~

"When Dorit first became ill, I thought she was having stomach aches until she finally told me she was also having a strange female drainage. In the beginning, I thought she meant her menses, for believe it or not, Dorit is not as old as she looks. Being a prostitute and ill has aged her more than 30 years."

"She began having a horrible milky drainage and her pains grew worse. Then she developed leg problems with small boils. Over time; the pains spread through her thighs and affected her insides. I don't know if you can tell, but she's having thought problems as if this disease is going to her brain. For the most part, she is quite lucid, but lately she forgets, or will repeat things, and there are times she does not remember things very well. She has been doing much better lately, but no matter what medicinal herbs and teas I use, nothing has worked. I spread a salve that I make over her body to ease the pain and try to keep her warm and comfortable."

"Dorit knew and finally told me about the sexual disease she was suffering from. She had stopped having customers come to the house and began sending them to one of the other ladies. She always told the women to look the man over before having them as a client, but sometimes early on the disease does not show itself.

Arbor took a deep breath and slowly moved around the kitchen area as he finished preparing the food and began setting out bowls and cutlery as the pot bubbled for the evening meal.

"The tables have turned for us and now I take care of her. She is no trouble and is grateful for any little thing I do for her. I have a small garden in the back with a section for my medicinal herbs and salves. I grow our own vegetables and even help care for the other ladies."

"Dorit never asked me to do any of this, but I enjoy the ladies and their company. I truly appreciate how they love my Dorit. Because of what they do, I make sure they, too, are cared for—in sickness and in health."

As his hands stopped moving, he turned to Tahmari and pointed to the chairs at the table.

"Dorit is asleep, but we can go ahead and eat. I also need to talk with you about some things that are pertinent to your new profession. You should know that I do not believe in your God, but if you'd like, you may say a prayer over this meal. Most of the ladies are not Jews but pagan believers, who have some knowledge and a bit of belief in your God through Dorit's teachings."

"There are many Jewish laws that prohibit you women from becoming prostitutes. This is a Jewish town and supposedly the men should not be frequenting the ladies, but they are like any other men and choose to keep them in business, for it is mostly the Jews who frequent these pagan women."

"I believe they feel that since they are committing adultery or fornicating with a pagan woman, they are safe from your religious laws. Some of the prostitutes' customers are single, but many are betrothed or married and are unfaithful to their own women."

Turning to look fully at her, he asked a relevant question.

~15~

"If the Jews know of your God's laws, why do they do this?"

Tahmari looked down and replied, "I cannot answer that, Arbor. There is good as well as bad in everyone. Some feel because Yahweh is not physically beside them that He will not see their sins, yet my God's presence is everywhere. There are men and women who continue to sin because they have not been caught in the act, yet say they live by the Laws of Moses and the Commandments. Some say empty prayers, give the required tithes and alms, and believe that's all there is to it."

"Religion is not what you do, Arbor, it is how your heart and your faith is strong, and what's inside of you. One of our prophets told us how to live. It is not always the money you give for alms or tithes, or how often you fast or even pray many times a day. He said Yahweh requires his people to act justly, to love mercy and walk humbly with Him.[1] This does not always happen among His people. Jews know the Law and the Commandments, for we are all schooled as babies to adulthood, but we tend to do as we please. It is one thing to have the knowledge, but another to live the way Yahweh would have us live. I don't know if that makes sense to you or not."

Arbor was silent for a time as he turned this information over in his mind.

"Yahweh gives us all free will to do what we want, but it is our will that guides us."

Arbor squinted toward her. "There was a time when a man would visit Dorit, not as a client, but just to discuss with her about your Yahweh. He was very educated and they would discuss Jewish history and the Torah. He would read the scrolls to her and prayed for her health before he would leave. He was a good man and even helped settle some of the prostitutes' problems. She was very sad when she heard he had died."

Changing the subject, Arbor asked, "Tahmari, do you know about Jewish scrolls?" He turned his head and smiled. "Dorit talks about the scrolls and is educated, although most people, even the ladies, do not know that. I believe you, too, are educated, which is quite uncommon among females."

"Ah, Arbor, you are so astute. Yes, I know about the scrolls. When I next visit, I will bring a couple and read them to her!"

As she smiled at him, Arbor knew then she had received a good education.

"I have my uncle's scrolls and will come back and read and discuss them with Dorit, for I believe we will both enjoy hearing Yahweh's words. I promise. Please do not tell anyone I can read. A few of my uncle's friends know, but they had been sworn to secrecy and many have since died. There was a time when his friends would come to the house and they would read the scrolls to each other, but as a female I was not allowed to be in the room with them. I would sit outside the room and listen. In the evenings, I would always read the scrolls and tell scriptural stories to my aunt and uncle and it was an enjoyable time."

"I love Dorit and it will be good to be around another Jewish woman who understands Yahweh's word. I'm glad you told me that Dorit was educated also. Perhaps it will soothe her pain, or at least take her mind off her pain as she listens."

Arbor nodded his head as he headed toward the brazier and began scooping the meal into their bowls.

"Yes," he said, "I believe it will."

~16~

As she pulled chairs toward the table for the two of them, she questioned, "Have you no god you believe in, Arbor?"

He hesitated as he tried to give an answer she would understand.

"I was never introduced to one I wanted to have faith in. My master's god was not one I wanted to worship, for they believed in sacrificing babies and bowing toward foolish statues. I would most likely have had to follow his example and such worship would be a lie. Yet, my master never forced me to do so. In fact, I was never sure he himself believed in his own god, but his nation believed only in what they could see – the moon and stars, wood and brass, silver and gold – stupid things."

"I know you Jews believe in a God you cannot see or touch. I honor your God only because of Dorit. When she prays, I listen, but I cannot believe in Him, for I fail to see how you can believe in a god you cannot even see or touch. Yet you believe He hears your prayers."

"I have a friend, Najur, who I keep in contact with. We are from neighboring countries and he is also an eunuch. He is out of town now for he travels with his master. He prays to a god he calls 'the Creator' and he cannot see this god either, who seems to be similar to Dorit's. When he visits, the two of them like to sit and converse about their gods."

"Najur says the Creator created everything. Supposedly in a week or fortnight's time, he created the sun, moon stars, waters, even animals and humans, but Najur does not pray to nature or stars. He says we should not worship the creation, only the Creator. I don't know who this Creator might be, but Najur truly believes in Him. Truthfully, his god sounds pretty much like your God, one you cannot see or touch, but since I don't believe, I just listen and don't question him."

"In my country, my people worshipped the stars and the sun and moon. I never really believed in those gods either but I was too young to really figure that out. If I had not been taken away from my own homeland, I probably would have eventually believed in the gods of my nation."

"I know you pray, but it seems your God has not seen fit to answer your prayers or you would not be here, and for all her belief, Dorit would not be in the condition she's in."

"It is not that I don't believe in your God," he continued, "for I know Dorit does have faith in Him. She tells me stories from her Jewish history, about the Red Sea escape from Egypt, Jewish laws, and about an area beside the Jordan River where the people were able to take over a city just by walking around it."

"She also told me about a man who was supposed to walk around a city and talk to them about his God. That man refused in the beginning and got swallowed by some type of great fish. Eventually he did what he was supposed to do. I believe it is probably a children's story."

"She prays to Him, but He has not answered her prayers either, and He has not helped with her sickness. She loves this God and says her God loves her, but I cannot see that love if she continues to get worse."

Tahmari gave a slight smile. "You are right, Arbor. I have prayed, and as you say, my God has not found fit to answer my prayers either, otherwise my uncle would still be alive and I would not be in my own predicament. I believe in Yahweh through my faith in Him."

"However, I will teach you about my God, for my uncle taught me that it takes faith to believe. If you wish, when I read the scrolls to Dorit, I will also make sure I explain my Yahweh to you. Although it may not seem so to you, I do honor Him and I believe He understands my situation. Yet, as a Jew, I know I would be stoned, killed, or burned according to our Laws against fleshly sins."

Tears came to her eyes, but she blinked them away. No matter what, she thought, I still believe in Yahweh and know He has better plans for me, but I just don't see them right now.

She then bowed her head and said a prayer of thanks over the meal and requested the Lord to bless Dorit and Arbor.

~17~

After the meal, Arbor began explaining how she should talk to her customers, giving her hints on how not to feel a lot of pain the first time, and how she should take time to rest between customers.

He explained that prostitutes should always wear veils that only show her eyes and to not take it off on her business days. It is best that they wear their veils when they are with a man, and even when they travel outside of their homes. Veils must be distinctive and only show the eyes.

Tahmari never knew there were so many rules to follow.

He told her about pre-insertion and how to cleanse herself between customers. He gave her hints on hygiene and even how to apply the kohl to her eyes and lips. Once she had 'serviced' the man, she should never allow him to fall asleep in her house, but send him on his way. She should always count the money she makes and never leave it out in the open.

"There are men who will use you and try not to pay you. We both know you're in this profession for the money so make sure you are paid before you do anything. Don't let anyone take advantage of you. If you don't trust any man who comes to you to be serviced, give the excuse that you are at the time of your menses. They will leave you alone if you are believable. You can always hold your stomach as if you're having stomach cramps. Men don't want a woman who is in pain unless they've placed the pain on you themselves, so be careful."

"Oh yes! There are women who are deviants. Beware of them also. Never let a woman of that type come to your door, for sex between women is ridiculous! There are a few pagans who will have sex with them because those women will pay a lot more money for such favors. They are not friends with Dorit, for she abhors such behavior."

"On the days you need to rest, move your curtain across the doorway. All Jews know what that means. If it looks as if you are about to entertain someone you don't trust or who you know to be abusive, close the door. Stand behind the door and explain that you are not taking customers today. Seldom will a man try to force himself on you. They'll just go to the other side of town and seek out another prostitute."

"You are a good looking young woman and there are many of the town's harlots who are beginning to look their ages. Makeup can only do so much. Use olive oil on your skin to keep at bay the wrinkles as well as to remove makeup. Then wash your face thoroughly. I will supply you with a concoction I have recently made and have given to the others to help keep kohl from staying inside your pores and drying your skin."

Arbor reached inside a small bag on his waist and gave Tahmari a few coins.

"This money is from Dorit, to help you start your work. Take the money and purchase a few robes which open from the front. Do not pay a lot for them because you will not keep clothes on your body for long." At this, Arbor gave a lecherous smile.

Arbor then gave a demonstration of how she should sexily remove her robe and show her body to her customers. He tiptoed and pranced around the room, showing a feminine side she had not seen before. Her eyebrows rose to her forehead but she did not say anything. And without saying anything, he understood the question she did not ask.

"No, my dear, I have never participated in those games. Some eunuchs are known to become male prostitutes to men and women, but I have never participated in such. There are young men and women, as well as the elderly, who try to solicit deviant sex from eunuchs. Few will perform such acts. I know of this, but I do not know those eunuchs."

"My master was manly and had two concubines, so I was never asked to do anything of that sort. I have, however, watched Dorit when she was still working and was able to copy her mannerisms. We eunuchs are great mimics. You would do well to have the other ladies, especially Kiri, show you their mannerisms, how to dress, and how to apply the makeup."

After the meal, Tahmari stood and began collecting their bowls and eating utensils, but Arbor put his hand on arm.

"I do such things here. You can clear your own plates when you go home. Now, it is time for you to leave. I have put together a small package of food for you. Give yourself a day or so to heal from today's experience, for your first customer will be coming to you soon."

With those parting words, Tahmari left Dorit's home to begin writing down everything Arbor had told her. Before this time, she had believed it would be best to not divulge the fact that she could read, write and figure. Uncle Josiah had once told her that women were not supposed to know – it was only for men to know such things. Women were to only learn about housekeeping, yet Uncle Josiah still took it upon himself to give her an extensive education. She believed Arbor would keep her secret.

Looking behind her she noticed the same little dog. Has that dog always followed her or was she just now really noticing him?

~18~

He was younger than she thought he would be, but behind him was an even younger man. The older one's beard was not long or gray but his face was handsomely mature. The other man was younger and she could see he was a bit fearful. Like her, she believed the younger man would be her first and it seemed he was afraid and embarrassed.

How does a prostitute go about performing for her first time? Everything she had been told by Arbor went out of her mind and she became tongue-tied. Seeing her hesitation, the older man spoke first.

"Kiri said for me to bring this young 'isch' to you because the others are busy tonight. You don't look old enough to be doing this. I generally seek out my friend Kiri for the young men when it is their first time, but she's busy."

Whispering, he said, "This young man does not expect a lot out of you, so I'm quite sure he won't hurt you. I'll wait outside for him. I'll also pay you for a bit of conversation once he's done."

Putting his head down, he introduced himself but did not give the name of the young man.

"My name is Turza. The correct amount is there. Kiri has already told him your fee."

Tahmari was grateful for that because she never thought to ask Arbor how much she should charge. She would discuss this with Kiri tomorrow. The unnamed young man did not look lascivious at all and seemed as nervous of her as she was of him as she led him to the back room where she would do her business. Although her first time as well as his, there was some discomfort but they completed the act. She noticed he seemed satisfied when it was over.

She showed the man a small bowl and towel so he could clean himself, then went to the rear of the house to do the same. As both came to the front room, the young man silently nodded to her his thanks and went out the door with a smile on his face. In spite of herself, she smiled in return. The young man never uttered a word.

Turza came inside and sat at her small table. Slowly he placed another small money packet on her table as Tahmari sat. Her large eyes studied him as he studied her.

"You have feelings for Kiri?" she asked.

Turza quickly lifted his head. "You know that, how?"

"When you say her name, your voice drops and you have a flush. Have you made your feelings known to her?"

"No. She is not Jewish but I am. I'm quite sure she looks at me as if I am a false representative of our God. I believe she only believes in the Jewish God because of Dorit, for that lady teaches the women how to fit in with the people in the many cities and towns. Dorit knows Jewish history and scriptures. Her mother was Jewish, but her father was not."

"The women give their tithes, basically because Dorit tells them to do so, but they can only do so through someone else. The Temple priests do not allow the prostitutes to turn in their tithes, but most are pagan and find it unnecessary to give a portion of their earnings to the Temple, and an unknown god. If the women give their tithes to a Jewish man to contribute, their money would be accepted."

"You see, it is against the Mosaic laws and their money would be considered 'tainted'. Yet, if someone who is Jewish receives their tithes from them and submits it, it will be accepted. Some will turn it in as if their money was part of their own tithes."

Turza's voice was gentle and she appreciated his company for he wanted nothing from her, just small talk. He was well versed about the area and spoke of his travels. They sat across from each other as he discussed the area where he lived, speaking in a low voice about the weather and other mundane subjects."

She knew he was trying to make her feel comfortable in the presence of a man. He also gave her some advice which he felt she should be aware – most of which she had learned from Arbor, but she did not tell him that.

She believed Kiri had informed him the young man would be her first customer and requested Turza to take the man to her. Turza was also most likely told to stay a while in the event there was a problem.

Tahmari was quite sure Kiri knew Turza's feelings for her, but what were her feelings toward him? She did not know enough about Kiri to figure that out. When it came to her being a prostitute, she and Kiri could relate to each other, but otherwise she did not know her personal history or feelings.

As far as her personal knowledge of the other prostitutes for whom she had developed a friendship, she knew very little about them. Garner kept pretty much to herself, making sure she spoke slowly to cover her accent, whereas Luchi seemed to be highly intelligent, spoke Hebrew and Aramaic very well, but the most Tahmari had ever heard from her lips were to offer a few words of greeting or advice if asked, and whenever she spoke in Dorit's presence during their visits to their ill friend.

When Turza finally left her house she found he had placed a few added coins on the small stool. Tahmari was happy to meet someone who was nice, for she knew from Kiri and a few others that some men were rough—a few because they were in a hurry, some on purpose, and some because they did not know their own strength. She hoped she would never meet such men.

~19~

"What happened? What is happening?" Running to the front of the doorway, Arbor was frantic. He rushed toward Turza's side as the young man tenderly laid Kiri on the pallet Dorit used during the daytime. He handled the young woman carefully, knowing for sure she was comfortable before turning her over to Arbor's care. Going to the rear of the house, he produced two bowls and sat them on the table.

Tahmari had met up with Garner and Luchi and all three arrived with Turza and entered Dorit's house. The three women were trying to hold back tears as they looked at their friend.

Arbor stared at Kiri's face and wet a cloth to slowly wipe her bruises on the side of her mouth, her hands, and the front of her body. As he rubbed her skin with his medicinal yellow salve, he looked into the worried face of Turza. There was no doubt in anyone's mind that she had been badly beaten.

"I happened to be in the neighborhood, so I stopped by Kiri's house. Just to talk, mind you, just to talk." Turza stopped talking for a short time as he took a breath, but continued on.

"I heard sobbing and when I went inside, she was on the floor curled in a ball in a corner. She was almost unconscious, but she told me to take her to you, that you would know what to do. Then she passed out. The other ladies came with me to show me a much faster way to get here." He ended on a sob.

"You did right. She will now be in my care." Arbor's lips were tight.

He had moved the two bowls to a nearby stool and continued to wash Kiri's wounds. Arbor went to the back of the house to replace clear water in the bowls. Tahmari could see the anger in the eunuch's face as he placed a light coverlet over Kiri's body.

He turned to the other prostitutes.

"She is in shock. Do you know who did this to her?" All three women shook their heads.

Luchi answered. "Turza had Kiri in his arms when he passed Garner and myself on the way to wash clothes. Tahmari joined us on the path. We told him we needed to get Kiri to Dorit's house right way, so we showed him the back way we travel to avoid the crowds and stares."

Leaning on a stick, Dorit came into the room. They could see the tears in her eyes as she looked at her young friend on the pallet. She turned toward Arbor as he went toward her, making room for his mistress on the opposite side of the pallet.

Dorit lifted the coverlet and felt from Kiri's face to her feet, nodding her head as she touched each area of her body.

"Arbor will take care of her. She is badly beaten and bruised but she will survive, for Kiri is a survivor. There are no broken bones, praise Yahweh!"

Dorit turned her face from Kiri and looked at the other three women, giving a silent signal. She then nodded to Arbor, who gave a responding nod and continued his ministrations. By this time a few more prostitutes came into the house for word had reached them also.

"Ladies, I need to speak with you all privately."

Luchi, Garner, Tahmari and the other women followed behind Dorit to the back room where Dorit slept. A few other prostitutes arrived and gave sympathetic murmurings as they also followed along.

~20~

In the meanwhile, Turza and Arbor went toward a corner of the room to speak privately. Arbor's dark face was grim.

"Turza, did Kiri tell you who did this to her?" he quietly asked.

"No, but I saw the man running from her house as I was walking there. I don't know his name, but I do know what he looks like. Arbor, I promise you I will take care of this matter. I'll make sure none of the other ladies will have to be bothered by him."

"Many such men feel they can treat the prostitutes any way they want. They don't consider the fact that these women bruise and hurt like any other woman. Makes you wonder if they beat their own women!"

Arbor nodded his head in understanding. "Do what you have to do. I have always known you have feelings for Kiri and I appreciate you bringing her here. Thank you for your concern for her."

"It's not just concern, Arbor. I have always had feelings for Kiri. To me she is not a prostitute, she is a lovely woman. I would do anything for her, but she feels since she is not Jewish, she refuses to return my feelings. I don't care that she is not of my faith, for I know she honors my God, and that is enough for me. I am not sure of her religion for she does not mention it to me, but I've watched her give alms and is known to help others in need."

"I don't always come to her for sex, for she's a good listener and I just love being around her. I sometimes pay her for the entire night so I can be her only customer."

"I've told her personal things I have never told anyone else. She knows and keeps my secrets. I have a small farm and my home is not in this area. I am not a rich man, but I am able to support a wife and even a family. The Lord has blessed me to prosper in many ways. Yet, the one thing I have prayed for, Yahweh has not allowed me to have. And that is Kiri."

As he said her name, Turza looked toward the pallet. Arbor was still angry, but he understood.

"Yet, it is not always the unbelievers, but the Jews who frequent these women. Then they want to have unnatural sex or beat them because their own women will not do what they want. Jewish or not, there are other ways to be heathen besides through one's religion or lack of religion.

As they continued their conversation, Kiri began to moan. Slowly her eyes opened and searched the room. The men turned toward her and both hurried to her side. She searched the faces of the two men and gave a small smile.

Arbor picked up the cup of a warm medicinal tea he had earlier placed on the small table and helped to lift Kiri's head as he urged her to drink from it. She made a face at the taste of the bitter drink, but drank most of it. Closing her eyes, she slowly returned to an exhausted sleep.

"That is a draught that will allow her to sleep without much pain. It is made of various herbs from my garden. From the looks of her hands and arms, she put up quite a fight. A few of her nails are broken. Her attacker should show some bruises himself. She does not have any broken bones, but the bruises on her face and arms will take some time to disappear. She will stay here for a few days so I can keep an eye on her."

Turning toward the younger man, Arbor nodded his head and said, "Again, Turza, I thank you."

Arbor then stood, bowed toward him and silently left the room.

Turza went over to Kiri's sleeping form, sat on Arbor's stool beside the bed and held one of her hands, watching her as she slept.

~21~

"I know I do not have long, but what happened to Kiri is not uncommon." Dorit's voice was grave and tired.

"As you know, I am a non-practicing Jew. Perhaps I should not say 'non-practicing,' but this is only due to the fact that I am not allowed in the Temple. I try to follow the Law and the Commandments, give my tithes, fast and pray. The only Commandment I have ever broken is my occupation. The only other Jew in this room is Tahmari," Dorit turned her head toward her, "and you all know what the Jewish Law says about our profession."

"Prostitutes must keep their faces covered even as you accept a man into your house. In fact, I've known some men who don't even know the face of the woman next to them in bed and could pass her on the street and not know her identity."

"I'm sorry, my dears. I hope I am not repeating myself, for my mind comes and goes. If I do, just forgive me."

Dorit took a deep breath attempting to quell a cough, and sipped a bit of water before continuing.

"My advice to you is this: If you do not feel a situation is safe, you should leave your home. Come here should you have to do so. Men, in general, will sometimes demand more than what a woman is willing to give. Keep a weapon somewhere near you that you can reach in the event there is a problem. You have the right to turn someone away should they ask for a sex act you find repulsive – and there are many such acts."

Slowly she looked at each woman. "No matter how broke you might be, do not, I repeat, do not accept a relationship with a man who is diseased. Against my better judgment, I did so and look at me now."

"If there is a man who wants to marry you and you believe he will treat you well, consider the offer. The life we live should not be the only part of our existence. I had such an opportunity and turned it down. Instead the man gave me this house and Yahweh has still blessed me."

"I will not complain because He has blessed me with your love and friendship, the love and care of Arbor, and I am at peace."

"Many of you may remember Burlaht, I am quite sure," she stated quietly. A few of the older women responded with nodded heads or a quiet 'yes'.

"The rest of you need to know her story. She's dead now, but I feel her story should be shared with other prostitutes so you will not make the same mistake."

Slowly Dorit stood, grabbed her walking stick and headed toward the back of her house and, one by one, the women followed behind. Reaching the door, she stepped aside for them to continue to the rear of the house and pointed to three small mounds that had a bit of grass growing. They each had one small patch of flowers coming out of the soil. At the head of each one was a stone with etched markings.

"Those little mounds are graves, my dears. They are three baby graves put there by Burlaht. Burlaht did not keep track of her menses and became pregnant three times that I know about."

That first infant," she pointed at the closest mound, "one of her clients wanted to keep, even though he did not know if the child might or might not be his. It was his intent to rear the child as his own, for his wife was barren. However, the wife did not want to have in her house what she called a pagan baby, and although the baby was fully formed, it was born still, so that took care of the man's request."

"The second baby was miscarried. Yet, I believe that for some reason Burlaht would have kept that one herself had it lived. She never told me that, but I just had a feeling. I tried to help her keep track of her menses, until I realized she wanted a child of her own. Having a child is not good for business in our line of work, but it was her intent to quit and move on with the child, for it was also her intent to make another life for herself."

"She labored for two days for the last child. The midwives did everything they could to help, but Burlaht died trying. After she breathed her last, the midwives realized the baby had also died."

"Before she died, she had instructed one of the midwives to bring the babe to me to make sure I gave her infant a good home or a decent grave. Although I did not need a child in the house, I would have secretly made sure a good Jewish family who wanted a baby would raise it. We found where she had buried the other two and Arbor and I brought them all to this small area to give them a final resting place."

"If you look closely, you'll see where Arbor placed writings on the stones on top of each of their graves, as well as the flowering herbs. I really don't know what the stones say because they are written in his native language, nor do I know what type of herb is growing there. I do know that Arbor has never picked the herbs from the graves, nor has he ever planted seeds. Yet, each year the little flowers grow there and have never wilted or died. I have never asked what he named each infant and am aware only that the first one was a boy and the last was a girl."

Giving a huge sigh, Dorit studied each of the women in the room.

"I can tell you no more, but again, keep track of your menses. Yes, we know we are all prostitutes, but having a bunch of babies is not good for business or for our bodies. Don't let any man take advantage of you, or allow them to use and abuse you."

Dorit looked sad for a moment, then lifted her head and smiled at her friends.

"Try your best not to develop feelings for your customers. For that is what they are, ladies. Whether you call them clients or even patrons, if you wish. They are still your customers."

"I can tell you no more, but please remember my words and what I have taught you about my God. I have been praying for you all. I'm telling all of you to remember that if you meet a man who does not mind the fact that you are a prostitute and wants to marry you, consider his compassion as you consider him. Don't be hasty in your decision, but make sure you wisely consider it."

Using her walking stick, Dorit re-entered the house, went toward her bed and began to slowly ease herself to sit on the edge. The women took this as a sign to leave. As they returned to the front room, they saw that Kiri was resting comfortably and Turza was holding one of her hands. Arbor was on the side cleaning the area. He turned toward the women and nodded as each of them left the house.

~22~

"No, I am sorry to say, I did not bring any servants with me. I traveled with one of my head servants and two others, but they have returned to watch over my property. This trip is to give myself time away to transact the business of my animals, get some much needed rest, and see the various towns around Judah and Jerusalem—a sort of vacation, you might say. I do, however, know how to fend for myself since I was the youngest and only boy among five sisters."

"To get me out of their hair, they took time to teach me what they were being taught by my now deceased mother."

Aheelim chuckled to himself. "Not only do I know how to cook and clean, but my youngest sister even taught me how to make colorful dyes. She loved bright colors and I helped her when she would work with linen."

"We had servants, but because I was always curious, underfoot and getting in their way, they also taught me how to be a 'male servant,' for they taught me how to wait on them hand and foot," he smiled at the memories.

"Of course this certainly worried my father. Although I was young, he quickly began allowing me to work with him to perform duties to help him and how to run the family business. He also sent me to the Jewish school when I was of age to be around other males and learn things every good Jewish boy should know. I believe he wanted to make sure I did not turn into a girly-boy."

"I'm happy to be in this area near Jerusalem for the Festival of Booths. We have always celebrated this festival in my area, but not the way it is celebrated here. The many booths are marvelous—each one more expressive than the other!"

The owner of the small house smiled at Aheelim. Ah, he thought, a man who knows how to do his own domestic work. He could tell the man was not from this area for he knew that well-to-do Jewish men made sure they either hired a housekeeper if they were without a wife or servant, or would come to town expressly to find a wife.

If that was so, generally there came with him someone from his family who helped in picking the right girl. This man looked wealthy, carried himself well, and would be a great catch for some girl if he chanced to begin looking for a wife.

"Many Jews outside of this area seem to be able to fend for themselves, I notice. Should you require servants, let me know. You should be aware that there are cooking utensils, pottery, blankets and other household items on the small shelves in each room. A supply of kindling is beside the hearth and there is a clean brazier for your use, as well as more wood behind the house. Although this place looks small, it has large rooms that I believe you will find satisfactory should you wish to entertain."

He had Aheelim sit at a wide table to discuss business. After accepting the money, the landlord clapped for the three young menservants he brought with him to help unpack Aheelim's horse and mules and place those items in the appropriate rooms.

The landlord sent one of his men with the unpacked animals to the livery area to inform the livery master the animals' owner would be along later to complete the business of stabling his animals.

Within a quarter hour, the landlord returned to Aheelim and proceeded to finish their business. He gave Aheelim directions to the livery area and a nearby inn to purchase a decent evening meal.

"If there is nothing else, kind sir, enjoy your stay," he said as he bowed. Giving a signal he and his servants headed toward the door.

It did not take long for Aheelim to familiarize himself with the house and later take a nap. He awoke much refreshed a few hours later, said his midday prayers, and decided to take a walk to become familiar with the area.

First, he went to the Temple, offered a sacrifice to thank the Yahweh for his safe journey, and purchased a few food items from the street merchants on which to nibble as he walked around the marketplace, later purchasing more food for the next day. He then found the livery area, met the livery master and paid him for the month, saying he would pay for his services on a monthly basis for the rest of the time he would be in town, which would probably be a bit over a year.

Satisfying himself that he could always find his way back to his rented house, he returned there and worked on his business papers, later eating a light evening meal, and settled down for the night.

~23~

The twins, Jaffal and Jakri, had noticed the newcomer walking around the marketplace a few weeks prior, and after seeing him again later, decided to speak with him.

The brothers found him personable and at first glance believed he was somewhat naïve. Yet, it did not take long for the two to realize Aheelim was not as naïve as first perceived, for in conversation he seemed to be more businesslike than men his age.

And from his conversation, they could also see he was well-read. Silently they admired his dress and his walk for, as they observed, it was that of a man of authority, possibly in connection with the area from whence he came.

In retrospect, to Aheelim's eyes, the two men seemed to be somewhat childlike. They constantly used their hands as they spoke with him and one another.

One brother would start a sentence and grope for a word, but the other would voice the word and continue the conversation. They both smiled and giggled like young girls, but he found them friendly enough. They talked so much they never asked his name or where he was from, but addressed him as 'kind sir.'

A few times after that they would see him on the road and hurry toward him to create a conversation. On one occasion, they went to a small inn which had benches outside and ate a light lunch of dark bread, smoked fish, cheese and fruit, along with cups of unfermented wine.

Since he was the one who suggested they stop for the mid-day meal, Aheelim paid for the three of them. At their wide smiles, he became aware that they carried no money or script, which he found unusual for adult Jewish males. He, as well as the innkeeper, noticed they were careful to eat their fill and not leave a crumb behind. The innkeeper smiled and gave Aheelim a knowing wink as he removed their plates while picking up the money that was placed on the table.

Nonetheless, Aheelim enjoyed listening to their prattle for they were informative about the area and could describe the many booths which lined the roads from the city of Jerusalem and various towns surrounding it.

The sky was clear showing few wispy clouds in the distance and, being full from the meal, their walk became a lazy but comfortable stroll.

~24~

They came upon a series of small houses on the outskirts of town and Jaffal explained they were nearing the area where the prostitutes conducted business. Some of the women sat fanning themselves outside their doors and stared at them over the tops of their veils. A few were conversing in small groups or doing household chores, while others ignored the three men. There were a few small abodes which reminded Aheelim of the cave areas in his home town.

"Most of them are pagan," explained Jakri. "They are nice prostitutes and many them are very clean, and they do a good business in the evenings. They've been getting a lot of business from those who traveled to the main Temple at Jerusalem for the services."

"Jew or pagan, the men don't really care. If one is busy or not able to service you, there is always another one available."

The two men prattled on. "My brother and I like to use the same woman." At Aheelim's strange look, Jakri corrected himself.

"Oh, no, not at the same time, mind you, but we are friends to a few of them. We generally go to our favorites and then attend the city baths to clean up. Best to do so, I always say. Can't be too sure, you know? Hahaha!"

He gave a nervous giggle as he turned toward his brother.

"Just because they look clean, doesn't mean they always are, right Jaffal?"

Both men became a bit more serious when Jaffal noticed Aheelim did not seem too pleased with the conversation and gave a strange look toward his brother, who took the hint, and changed the subject to a more mundane topic.

They pointed out buildings of interest in the town, the new park area Pilate had opened to families and recommended another inn close to Jerusalem City which had nice rooms available and served good food, whose menus they suggested Aheelim might wish to sample.

Aheelim realized this was more for their own benefit than his own.

As the men rounded the corner and headed back toward the center of town, a well-dressed man was coming toward them.

"Ah, here comes our good friend, Samtil. He's friend to the high priest and one of our town's officials, and he is a great one to know."

Introductions were quickly made and general conversation ensued. Aheelim noticed they referred to him as their "new friend."

Samtil found the visiting man personable and after welcoming Aheelim to the town, he excused himself for having to hurry away, saying he was busy but would plan to meet with him at another time. He quickly left the men and Aheelim noticed it seemed as if his mind was otherwise occupied. It sounded as if the man was mumbling something about a Rabbi who keeps teaching near the Mount who was disputing the Mosaic laws and how the stupid people tended to flock toward any rooster that happened to scratch across the road.

"What is that all about?" he wondered.

After awhile, Aheelim announced he was on his way toward the stock areas where there were sheep, horses, cattle and camel sales on the outskirts of town. Nodding his thanks to the men for their company, he then took his leave.

Looking over his shoulder, he watched the twins as they headed toward the merchant and tradesmen areas. He was sure that since the two carried no coins or a script bag, they were not going there to purchase anything.

Aheelim left the stockyards after a few hours and headed toward his rented house, mentally setting up his calendar as to whom he would be meeting within the next few weeks and months. He had traversed the town earlier after finding the stock areas where he would be meeting with buyers of his animals. He had more than a few months' worth of business meetings to attend and he needed to rise early in the morning to figure out where the various businesses were located.

It was bad manners to be tardy when one wanted to conduct business and he was not one to show up tardy to any of the meetings.

~25~

"Good day," Eliah nodded to Aheelim. "I'm sorry I have not been able to spend time with you since you arrived in town. We've met in the stockyards and spoke in passing, but never one on one like today"

"Good day to you." Aheelim remembered this quiet man when he was near the sheep pens.

"I'm in town to transact some business and was on my way to the Temple. Someone told me the healing Rabbi was on his way to town, but I overheard the women near the well conversing that the Teacher has not yet come into the town proper. You see I was hoping to hear him. I've been told many good things about Him and His healing powers. I've heard He has power from the Almighty, which is how He is able to heal."

Walking in step with the newcomer, Eliah introduced himself. "I pray you enjoy your stay here. I, too, am heading that way. I have not personally met the Rabbi, only to see Him from a distance, but have heard of his miracles and have met with people who have been recipients of healings by Him."

"Yesterday I was able to speak with a man who said the

Rabbi healed his blindness. I do know he was truthfully blind for I would see him sitting by the gates begging alms, and when I saw him again, he was walking toward me and able to see. I used to place alms in his bowl and prior to that I never saw him blink. His eyes used to be cloudy but now they are clear."

"What do you feel about this Man?" Aheelim was curious as to how people felt about Jesus. "Do you feel He could be the long-awaited Messiah?"

"I have not really formed an opinion of Him as yet. I know many of the officials and priests feel He's a charlatan. Having seen Him only a few times, I don't see anything of his character out of the ordinary, but I have heard of His healing miracles. Only Yahweh is able to do such things, as if the Man was given such power by Him."

The two men stopped beside a blacksmith shop. Eliah's eyes traveled toward the people walking in the streets. He placed his hand on Aheelim's arm and turned to look him in the eye.

"Do you remember hearing from your parents about a man who professed to be the anointed one—about 20 or 25 years ago—a Galilean, who had many followers? He was said to be the messiah, but when he gathered a lot of followers, Roman leaders of that time dispatched guards who chased him and his followers away? There was another one later, who never professed to be the Christ, but he also gathered many around him. The Romans used harsh punishment in breaking up the crowds and that man disappeared for a time. My mother told me she remembered that many people were executed by the soldiers, and a few years later, that false messiah was finally located and executed without a trial."

"It's very strange, for although this new Rabbi gathers a great many followers, no riots have ever broken out by the people. Nor has He claimed to be the messiah. I have noticed the crowds are quiet and listen intently to Him, which is probably the reason why the Romans do not attempt to disperse them."

"As you know, the families of Herod were raised as Jews, yet they are still ruthless toward us. That was probably why his father was made ruler over Galilee and later Jerusalem. To get back at the Jews who followed those false messiahs, the authorities retaliated by raising all of the people's taxes."

"Rome does not like a lot of Jews gathering in crowds, for it is their belief that crowds or too many Jews together may be prone to start an uprising against Roman authority. Rome has already expressed that the Jewish religious laws should control us, which gave authority to the priests and scribes to exercise judgment over the people. The high priest and the Sanhedrin rule such problems, not the Roman government."

"I am finding the problem today is not the Roman authorities, but the Temple priests, scribes, and town officials who are against this Jesus, for He preaches a different message. I'm not sure where the 'Kingdom of Heaven' might actually be that He always teaches, but His message seems to carry one major theme."

Eliah made excited gestures with his hands and tapped each of his fingers. "This Jesus has one theme: Love. Love of Yahweh. Love for each other and love for our neighbors."

Showing surprise, Aheelim asked, "You've heard Him speak in person? You've seen Him?"

Eliah smiled. "Oh yes, but not up close or personally. I try not to express my belief in this Rabbi quite yet, because it was only a few times. I have spoken personally with a man whose sight was returned, and have been in conversation with many tradesmen who have seen His miracles."

"But I have my own beliefs. I just don't say anything for or against Him because so many of the town's officials, priests, and even my friends are against Him."

"Until this Nazarene does something against Roman rule, He's safe. The priests and town officials here feel the Rabbi may be plotting an uprising. Yet, the Rabbi gathers three or more times as many followers as the fake messiahs and the crowds of people are never dispersed by the Romans. In fact, when I heard Jesus speak north of here, there were Roman and Temple guards in the audience who sat and listened just like the rest of us."

Eliah shook his head sorrowfully. "I really like this Man, and I'm afraid it will not be the Romans who will go after Him, but the Jewish Council. They've never had competition like this before. Yet, I believe that is not the Rabbi's purpose, for His message is simple."

"A friend of mine said Jesus told them He did not come to change any of Yahweh's laws and commandments. He seems to be teaching the right things and has never tried to refute Yahweh's Word."

"Well," Eliah scrutinized the sun's rays as he said, "I'm looking at the time and will leave you now. I know I've talked my head off, but you're a likable young man and I appreciate the time we've had in conversation."

Nodding his head, Eliah bid Aheelim goodbye and both continued toward their separate destinations. Aheelim realized that like the twins, this man never asked his name, but he also did not volunteer it.

~26~

When Aheelim came out of the Temple a few days later, he met up with Samtil, the official who was introduced to him by the giggling twins a few weeks ago, finding his greeting friendly. They walked around the square, past the water wells, and very close to the community the twins had pointed out as the 'prostitutes' neighborhood'. It was still early in the day so very little business was being conducted.

Yet, he found the entire area was also an area of commerce, for there were a few merchants with cheap wares on their carts, a few sellers of fruit, cooked fish, bread, goat's milk and wine, as well as a stand of cheap sandals, scarves and jewelry. An old cart ambled past the men that sold material and multi-colored balled yarn. They moved to the side as an old woman driving a merchant's cart, rolled past them yelling out something in a foreign language. A few of the prostitutes came forward to check out her wares.

Aheelim noted that the street on which they were walking had an odd aroma – fish, old vinegar, cooked meat, and cheap perfume.

Samtil wrinkled his nose and commented, "It's bad

enough there are prostitutes around the town, but some are too close to the sacred areas."

"Most of those women are pagan, but there are a few Jewish women who have started having men frequent them as well. Between the prostitutes and that Nazarene, Jesus, things are really changing in this town."

"Jesus?" Aheelim's ears perked up. "Who is Jesus exactly? Are you speaking of the Teacher himself or one of the dozen men who follow him? If this is the same man I've been hearing about, He seems to do good wherever he travels. I believe the men with him are his disciples. I have heard how he heals the infirmed, causes the blind to see, and an oriental trader recently told me how a demon-possessed man was released from his demons. It seems to me He is going about doing nothing but good works. Only Yahweh could have bestowed on him such power."

"Ah, you don't know, do you?" Samtil was quick to explain why he spoke of the man with disdain.

"He seems to have some type of spiritual power that He feels allows Him to heal on the Sabbath, meet and eat with sinners, and then, of all things, the people declare him to be the 'son of God'! That, in itself, is blasphemy. He teaches contrary to what is taught in the Temple. Many of the priests and town's leaders are against him."

Aheelim could see Samtil's displeasure in his purpling face as he continued to huff and puff.

Aheelim was not of an opinion yet since he'd never

seen or heard the Rabbi in person, but the more he heard of Jesus and His ministry, the more he believed the opposite of what Samtil was spewing. He knew he would have to judge for himself and not pass judgment by what he was hearing from this man, whose background he barely knew.

Realizing he did not have enough information to voice an opinion, he then changed the subject.

"Do you have a large family?" he asked his walking companion.

Samtil was caught off guard by the question and sputtered a bit. Aheelim noticed he was a bit older than himself, perhaps 32 years old or so, and dressed as one who had authority and money. Based on what the twins had recently relayed to him, Aheelim knew he was a town official and very well known. Although somewhat on the chunky side, he was solidly built, had a well-trimmed beard and could even be considered handsome in a strange way.

"No," he answered as he calmed down. "I wanted to become betrothed to one young lady a few years ago, but her uncle felt she should have someone much younger. I do not consider myself old, but I would like a young wife who can give me sons, yet at that moment it was not to be. The uncle has since passed on and I don't know what happened to his niece. She is probably married with several children by now – for this happened some years back."

"I know there are men who would like to set up a

betrothal contract with me for their daughters, but I have no feelings toward any of them. I also know the fathers are seeking security for them, but the ones who would like to have me for a son-in-law have daughters who are not very comely and most of them titter so much that it becomes an irritant."

"That is not to say the girl must be beautiful, mind you, but the one for whom I offered had beauty, wit and a pleasing personality. These other girls seem to be nothing but simpering fools and agree with everything I say because that is how they were raised. I also don't want a loose woman, for I already see enough of that around here – what with all the prostitutes in town, as you can observe."

The official said this as he waved his arm around the area, pointing out a few prostitutes.

They continued leisurely walking until Samtil took his leave and Aheelim turned toward the road that led to where he boarded his livestock.

For some strange reason Aheelim was not sure he trusted the official. It wasn't so much what he said, but his attitude. There was something about his attitude that made him uneasy. He believed Samtil had more than a personal knowledge about the prostitutes, but then, that was his own opinion. Sometimes a man's character was determined by his environment — the rabbi who schooled him in his youth, as well as his parents, his friends or even his home or town.

~27~

Aheelim continued toward the livery road and, turning the corner saw a large-boned fruit and vegetable merchant pushing a man against his wagon while holding a long knife in his hand against his captive's neck.

He could see the captive was a young man – no more than 23 or 24 years of age, perhaps younger – and very afraid. He was dirty, wearing only a short loincloth and a ragged shirt, with hair that was also ragged, matted, and long. He was not as dark as many of the slaves he'd seen in the area, but because of his unkempt appearance, it was hard to tell his complexion or where he hailed from.

The merchant was screaming at his victim as he waved a huge knife while there was abject fear in the young man's eyes.

As Aheelim ran toward the two men, he began waving his fist in the air while yelling, "Here, here! What's all the commotion about? What goes on here? What are you doing with my slave?"

Both men turned toward him, although the merchant never moved the knife away from the young man's neck.

The merchant began yelling back, "You have nothing

to do with this, sir, for I caught him stealing food from my cart!"

Aheelim could see that the captive's eyes were silently imploring him for help. He was aware of a brand on the man's thigh, which showed he was a slave – more than likely a runaway.

Without further thought, Aheelim continued running toward the couple while waving his fist in the air as if he was truly irate. Thinking quickly, he pretended to know the slave by giving him a name. For some reason or another, the only name that rushed to his mind was 'Goshen.'

"Goshen," he shouted, "What are you doing? Why did you leave me? Didn't I tell you to wait for me? Are you stealing? You scoundrel! I should let this man cut your head off. Do you hear me, come here! Come here!"

The merchant turned toward him without lowering the knife and adamantly questioned, "Does this man belong to you? He grabbed some of my food and was trying to run away without paying for it. He is a thief and everyone knows thieves deserve to be punished!"

As the merchant slowly lowered his weapon, Aheelim punched the slave hard on his boney shoulder as a master would normally reprimand his property and noticed the slave winced, which he found unusual for many slaves become hardened to being punched.

"I am sorry, sir," Aheelim began apologetically. "I

purchased this young man some time ago, and, yes, he belongs to me. I told him we would shop for food in the morning, but it seems he went ahead of me. He's never gone against my wishes before. I will pay for whatever he stole, and will be purchasing more food for my household as well. Let me settle his debt with you, but this will be a lesson to Goshen until we finish our business and get home, where he will be sorely punished. You can be assured this occurrence will not take place ever again!"

He turned toward the ragged man who stared as he gave the slave a slight wink. Surprised, the slave's eyes became huge, and now aware of what his rescuer was doing for him, he hurriedly responded. Turning toward Aheelim, he became contrite and lowered his body to kneel before him.

"I am so sorry, master," the young man mumbled, "but I lost sight of you and was hungry. He caught me because I did not have any coins to pay. Please do not be angry or beat me. I will not do it again, I promise."

Aheelim could see the merchant had been weighing what was said and finally moved the knife to his side, releasing the slave. Grimacing, the merchant grabbed one of his large burlap sale bags and shoved it toward the slave, making him hold it as his 'master' began filling it with figs, grapes, raw vegetables, a few blocks of cheese and barley bread.

The bag wobbled a bit for Aheelim could see the slave

was still overcome with emotion and fear, but his hands held tightly to the bag as Aheelim filled it with the food. He knew more than enough money was pressed into the merchant's hand for his purchase and what the slave had stolen. He also knew it was probably only a few pieces of fruit that was taken, but gave the merchant more than what would adequately cover the high amount he was quoted and for the groceries he was now purchasing.

Grabbing the slave, who was still holding tightly to the bag, Aheelim began pushing him in his back causing him to walk stumblingly ahead of him.

As they rounded the corner away from the merchant area, he pushed the slave against a nearby building while holding him around the neck and lifting him to the tips of his toes off the ground.

"I can see you're a slave and you and I both know your name is not Goshen. I called you that to save you, but are you a runaway?" he barked.

Fear returned in the slave's eyes as he nodded in the affirmative and lowered his head. Aheelim could see he was afraid of being beaten. Loosening his grip, he allowed the slave to stand on his own.

Motioning for the slave to walk with him, Aheelim began to ask him about himself. Finding a quiet area near an old grotto, they sat on two boulders. Aheelim reached inside and gave the man some fruit and a piece of the cheese.

"Eat it," he ordered. "I'm not going to beat you, but you need to know these tradesmen live by their own nation's laws. He would have gutted you like a goat in five seconds, and as a runaway slave, no one would have mourned you. What is your true name and where are you from?"

Quickly stuffing his mouth with the food, he chewed and swallowed quickly, almost to the point of choking. When he finally spoke, it was hesitant with an odd accent, but he seemed to be fluent in Aramaic.

"I was told I was born near Mount Shapher, which is very far from here, but my family and I were captured by traders when I was a child and we were all sold into slavery. I worked as a shepherd, then was apprenticed to a worker of silver when I was young, later a groomsman for my second master as well as his driver. I worked in a tannery and in the stables for my third master, but he died and his son had to sell me and others to my last master."

"I have had four masters since I was six, but my last master worked me in the fields. Because of my masters, I was able to learn different languages and became helpful to them in business when we traveled to various areas for trade. I was a good slave and worth much to him. Although I cannot read, I am good with figures."

"My last master was very mean to his slaves. He and his son would constantly beat me and my older brother without reason, finally beating my brother to death because he dropped a bowl. All the slaves were made to watch as they beat him. Those men enjoyed hurting us and it was then I knew that I would be next, so I waited for an opportunity to run away."

"My master had to purchase timber and needed many slaves to carry it back to his home so he brought me and others along. My chance for freedom came when we reached the outskirts of this town."

With a catch in his voice, he lowered his head so Aheelim could not see his tears, giving a noisy sob and hiccup before he continued.

"My name was always changed by different masters. The name my mother gave me was Jepthun. My true father was killed during the raid, but my mother became pregnant within the year by one of the raiders. She died of ill health three years after my baby sister was born."

"The baby stayed with us for some time, but another family purchased my sister, Elema, as a small child after my mother's death. I pray Elema is being well treated, for it was a woman who purchased her for her own daughter. If she is still alive, by now she would be about ten years old."

His chewing slowed down as his hunger was abated.

"My master's business took place in an area past here and as our caravan passed near this area, I decided it was time to run away. There are many people here so I felt it would be very easy to get lost in a town this size. I saw my master and his men searching for me a few days afterward, but he was on a tight schedule and they have since traveled on. I did not think it would be so hard to find food, but I have been fending for myself for almost a month."

"I truly did not see that man behind his wagon, for it looked as if the seller had moved away for a few minutes, possibly to relieve himself, which would have given me time to grab something and be gone. I was really hungry and did not give the consequence much thought. You see, I had not eaten for a few days and felt I could quickly steal some food from the cart, but he came out of nowhere and grabbed me. When I saw the knife, I knew I would be killed."

"In the beginning, I had been eating scraps that were being thrown away behind one of the inns, but was chased away by other men who also scavenged for scraps. I would wait until nightfall to drink water from the well in town so as not to be seen."

He looked thankfully at Aheelim. "I owe you my life, my lord, and will be your slave if you will have me."

Again, he bowed low toward Aheelim. Not knowing what to do next, Aheelim made him stand and instructed him to walk with him to his house.

Quickly preparing some of the food, he fed him from his larder along with some of the newly purchased fruit and vegetables. As he pushed a cup of goat's milk toward

Jepthun, the slave laid his head on the table and began to sob.

Aheelim was almost embarrassed and turned toward the area he used as a desk. He realized the man had a lot of pent-up emotions to release and let him cry in private for a short time.

When he felt Goshen's emotions were well spent, he walked slowly over to him and patted him on the shoulder.

"Er - um, I'll tell you what, young man. Just eat and rest a bit and we'll figure out something later. I have no need for a slave for I already have many servants in my home. Personally, I do not believe in owning another human being, but I also do not have anything against those who do."

"I've just been here some months in order to sell my animals and decided to stay for some time as a sort of vacation. I, too, am not from around here."

"When you are rested, we will go to the small stream near here so you may wash and clean yourself. I have a few sets of servant's clothing left by some of my men that you can wear, so at the very least you won't be so obvious."

Jepthun almost fell asleep while sitting up straight in the chair. Aheelim found an old face knife the slave could use for trimming his hair and beard, put a few hygiene items on a rough towel and poured water into a bowl. He nodded to the slave, signifying he should begin using the items he had laid out.

As he headed toward the door, he looked back at Jepthun and ordered, "I would advise you to not try running away. I'll be back in less than a few hours, so be here when I return. And don't try anything funny with the knife. It's for trimming your beard."

With that, Aheelim closed the door and went to check on his horse and mules. As he walked, he began wondering if he had done the right thing. After all, he did not know the young man, who had already shown himself to be a thief.

"Well I'm quite sure Yahweh will let me know," he thought.

Turning down the road toward the livery, he saw the two brothers as they crossed on the other end of the lane, but they did not notice him as they were gesturing and excitedly talking to each other.

"Good! I really don't want to be bothered with those two today," he thought. There was something about the two men which did not sit well with him, but he could not put his finger on what made him uneasy about the brothers. It was the same uneasiness he had felt earlier about the town official.

~28~

As he reached the livery, he met the livery master coming from the back barn area. He was flexing his arms and mumbling to himself. He looked up and saw Aheelim coming through the door.

"Ah, checking on your animals, eh, my lord? They are all just fine although I'm a little behind in grooming your horse, but he's been fed and watered. I'll put him in the pasture later to take exercise. My groomsman has been ill, and the other man got another job, so I'm doing a lot of the work myself."

"Well, Yahweh be praised!" Aheelim thought as he raised his eyes toward heaven. Turning toward the livery master, he made him an offer of help.

"I have just the answer to your predicament. I have a freed slave for which I have no use, but I would like for him to be able to work somewhere to make a living on his own. He's thin but strong and is used to hard work. He needs employment and I would be happy to bring him by in the morning, if that would help you."

"After I bring him, if you decide you don't need him, I'll take him back, but I heartily recommend him. Since he's not used to making money, whatever you pay would be good for him."

The livery master rubbed his beard as he took a moment to consider the offer, pacing back and forth while Aheelim waited. He could see the man was certainly in dire straits.

Rubbing the length of his beard, the livery master slowly said, "I can't pay him a lot, but I am desperate. My head groomsman is my sister's son and he's ill. His illness comes at a bad time for I have new customers bringing five or six horses and a few more mules first thing in the morning. I can certainly use the help. Any tips or extra coins your man receives from the customers will be his."

"Of course, I'll need a document from you showing the slave is free, but yes, I'll hire him on your recommendation."

"By the way, my name is Abner. I've been running this livery for the last 10 years after taking it over from my grandfather. It's a good living, and gives my relatives a bit of money by working for me."

He held out his hand and Aheelim gave it a firm clasp after introducing himself.

"You don't have to pay him much, just a few coins here and there. Just make sure he eats at least two meals a day. He can sleep in your loft and be security to watch over your animals at night. He used to be a groomsman, so he pretty much knows what to do. His name is – ah – I call him Goshen. As for my horse, I'll stay to exercise and groom him myself so that job will be out of your way."

Abner readily agreed with a smile.

After riding his horse to the edge of town for exercise, he returned and began grooming the animal. Then, making sure his animals were in good order, he had a genial conversation with the livery master and left to head home.

During that time, he mentally developed a plan to help the slave. He did not want to lie, but something had to be done. He surely couldn't have the man staying with him.

He hurried back to his house where he found Jepthun in the act of trimming his hair and face, wearing only his loincloth. He was surprised to see that although the man was tall and thin, he was very muscular and looked a lot younger than he had previously thought. Aheelim helped him trim his beard and hair, for he was sure the slave had never done so seeing he was somewhat clumsy with the knife.

He was surprised to see whip marks on his back and shoulders, noticing the purplish welts looked recent. The brand on his thigh was an ugly one, possibly not correctly placed by his last owner or perhaps placed over a previous one.

Pagan slave owners were known to mark their slaves to show ownership. There were also bruises on his shoulders which he thought may have been where the man had been beaten, causing him to understand why the slave winced when he punched him there.

The two later went to the stream where Jepthun spent some time relaxing in the water with a smile on his face. As he began bathing himself, Aheelim situated himself on a small ledge and told him about the job and his idea. As the slave left the water, he handed him a rough piece of material for the man to dry himself.

"Although your given name is Jepthun, you will now be called Goshen. Goshen was a place of refuge and safety for the Jews when they were slaves in Egypt."

Goshen looked at him with questioning eyes and it was then that Aheelim realized he had no idea of Jewish history. No mention had been made of the religions of his previous masters.

'I will draw up some papers as if I purchased you some time ago and later gave you your freedom. The livery master is a nice man and since you've had experience with animals, you would be an asset. His name is Abner and he told me he will be very busy with new customers who will arrive tomorrow morning, so he definitely needs the help. Plus, he will allow you to keep any extra money the customers give you."

"Once you start working for him, you must promise me you will not try to run away and, most importantly, NO STEALING!"

He emphasized these last two words by tapping his forefinger hard against Jepthun's chest.

"The way you look now is entirely different from when I first saw you. Should your old master return this way, just remain in the livery area and you'll be fine."

They returned to the house where Aheelim found and gave him a set of servant's clothing to wear and continued giving him instructions about his new job and how he should act around the customers.

Sitting down, Aheelim began writing a letter informing the livery master that he had purchased Goshen as a slave some time ago. He made up a name for the seller and, although right handed, he used his left hand wrote a wobbly signature. Then he completed the document to show he had recently freed him to work where he wished.

Bending beside the door, he rubbed the letter in the dirt and folded it back and forth so it would look as if the slave had been free for some time. He gave him an old script bag after placing the letter and a few coins inside. Goshen informed him that although he spoke a few languages, he was never taught to read so Aheelim read the document o him.

"Just remember, you are now Goshen, a freed slave. Oh, yes, and from now on, you don't have to bow before anyone any longer, for you are now a free man. Those coins should tide you over until you begin getting wages. I'll be living here for some time, so if you need me, don't hesitate to come back. It has already been a long day and is also past my midday meal, so we'll get something nourishing to eat and then let's both get some rest because you'll start your new job early in the morning."

Aheelim took Goshen to the same inn where he had eaten with the giggling brothers, and commenced to school him on what to expect in the new job. He also showed him how to eat a bit more properly instead of shoving the food into his mouth. Goshen watched Aheelim cut his meat and vegetables into smaller morsels and followed suit.

When they returned to his rented house, he showed Goshen where he could bed down in the curtained room, but the man quickly removed his clothing, except for his loincloth, made up a pallet in a corner from the blanket and covers, and lay down. Without either man saying anything, this action informed Aheelim that Goshen was not used to a regular bed, for within minutes he had fallen asleep.

Aheelim smiled and began preparing himself for bed. Later, while lying in bed, he realized he had become a trusting soul. He knew nothing of the man's character, had given him a knife, and now the man was sleeping in his house. He gave a silent prayer of thanks for protection and asked Yahweh to help him in getting the slave settled in the morning.

~29~

Goshen awakened before the sun had actually risen and looked around his corner area. As he stood, he stretched and realized he had never felt so free in his life. He quickly folded the pallet and blankets and put them in a corner. He then put on the clothes that Aheelim had laid out for him and found them to be a bit large, but he did not know that. Sniffing the material, he noted it was soft and smelled of heather and grass.

The clothes he previously wore were always too small but all the slaves he worked with wore similar clothing. If a slave died while in captivity, another slave would inherit that slave's clothes. It did not matter what the size might be.

The size of his new clothes did not matter to Goshen for he was able to move more freely and he liked the feel of the material on his skin and it had a smell similar to fresh fruit. Plus, there was a small pocket in the girdle of the leggings, which he presumed was to keep inside coins or notes from the master.

His rescuer had not yet risen, so he took two large water vessels from the back room and carried them to the town well. He lowered a bucket into the well and began drawing enough water to fill both of his containers.

Having completed filling his vessels, he prepared to leave when four giggling young girls approached, each holding a vessel for water. They looked similar and each had either one or two long braids down their backs. He supposed they were possibly sisters from one household.

After noticing how the four struggled to put the bucket into the well as they tried to draw the water, he placed his vessels on the ground and, without saying a word, proceeded to draw the water for them. The girls stood in awe of him, not saying a word, just staring at the tall man.

As the bucket was filled, he beckoned them to come closer. One by one, they stepped forward and allowed him to pour water into each of their vessels. After completion, he tapped the heads of each girl, picked up his own vessels and headed back to Aheelim's house. He could hear them yelling their thanks as he continued on his way. When he chanced to look over his shoulder, he saw them heading in the opposite direction carrying their vessels carefully so as not to spill a drop.

His sister, Elema, would have been around their age if she was still alive. He was sad for a moment but began to realize things were looking much brighter for him this day. Smiling to himself, he headed back toward Aheelim's house with a low whistle.

He was never allowed to whistle around his last master, and it felt good to be free enough to whistle whenever he wished.

~30~

Entering the house, Goshen found Aheelim dressed in a rich looking robe and had prepared something for both of them to eat before leaving.

"Are you ready Goshen? Let's eat a quick breakfast and then go see your new employer."

Looking at his water vessels, Aheelim smiled. "Thank you for the water." The ex-slave put his head down and nodded in return.

With the items he had set out for the ex-slave in his hands Aheelim watched as Goshen put the script bag in the pocket of his girdle and picked up a small burlap bag which contained a mid-day meal for later. Within 45 minutes, they were on their way to the livery and it did not take long to get there for it was still early morning.

"As soon as you can, be sure to give Abner your papers. It shows that I purchased you and you are now free. I doubt he will ask any questions, but if so, give a short bow and say I freed you because I had no need of your services. That is what he has already been told. I know you have skills, but let him see your work before offering any other information."

Goshen gave a smile and nodded in understanding.

The livery owner was in the process of registering three beautiful horses in his records – a chestnut, a roan and a young mare. He turned toward the newcomers, noting the man beside Aheelim.

"You're Goshen?" he asked and then nodded as he answered his own question upon seeing Aheelim.

"Ah, very good! There are four mules to be taken in back where there is grain and hay," he pointed, "and that other one needs to be taken to the back side of the barn. I'll be with you in a moment, but I need to finish with these men first."

Aheelim went to stand by his horse and patted its head as he watched Goshen nod his head and take the lone mule to the back of the barn. He seemed to know what he was to do as he picked up the reins of the mules, clicked his tongue, and led them to the rear. He returned minutes later with their bridles and hung them on a hook inside the door.

Abner smiled as he looked toward Aheelim. "Be with you in a moment," he repeated.

"I'm not in a hurry." Aheelim gave a short dismissive wave. "I'll leave you to your business and will return in about an hour. I want to speak with one of the stock merchants on the next street and will be back soon."

With that, he walked toward Goshen's direction as he went outside the door. He gave a short wave to him, who was busy spreading hay toward the mules. Goshen seemed to know what he was to do and gave Aheelim the biggest smile he'd seen yet.

~31~

He could not believe what he was hearing! Aheelim sat on the smooth log as he surveyed his special sheep. His shepherds were walking lazily through the small herd and waved at him. It was good to know his animals were in good hands for he had hand-picked these shepherds himself before embarking on the long journey. He saw the ewes had separated themselves and the frolicking lambs were beautiful, white and without blemish.

The stock merchant had wanted his sheep, but did not want to pay his asking price for them. It was Aheelim's goal to sell the ewes for a nice price and make a present of the lambs to the priests for Temple sacrifices, but it was this man's plan to purchase the entire flock at a lower price and thereby sell them outside the sanctuary to make a profit.

At first he thought the man must have been joking, but in continuing their conversation, he realized the man was the type that would offer shady deals to those who could barely afford to purchase such animals for sacrifice. Aheelim had conducted deals with his father as a youth and knew the type of person with whom he was dealing.

His father taught him to not make unwise deals with men of low character. He always told him and his sisters to search their hearts before they planned any type of alliance to see if it is a decision Yahweh would also be in agreement. He believed his sisters followed his father's advice, for they all agreed to their betrothals and marriages with this in mind.

As he thought back, it came to him that their father never set up any of his sisters' betrothals without checking with them first, for he let them pick their own husbands.

Tradition said the eldest would marry first, but his father allowed the middle sister to be the first to marry and then the older one.

He could still hear his father's warning to him as the man continued rambling, for he had quickly begun to tune out his words.

"My son, there are always schemers in this world. Pray and use your Yahweh-given gift of discernment when doing business and you'll never go wrong."

Aheelim brought his mind back to the present for the man was still smiling and talking.

"Come, come, my man, we can both make a profit. The people have to exchange their money for Temple coins in order to purchase sacrificial animals. Too bad you did not bring doves, for the poorer people tend to use them for their sacrifices."

The man had a curious gleam in his eyes as he gave a

lecherous chuckle. Aheelim did not fall for his suggestion. He may be young, but he was very aware of men who tended to cheat the poor.

"No," he stated adamantly, "I have a purpose for the ewes and their lambs, for they are without blemish. I do thank you for your offer."

The stock merchant looked at him in surprise, but said nothing, for he could see Aheelim was not planning to change his mind.

As he walked away, Aheelim felt there was no need for the man to know about the unblemished doves he had previously given to the Temple priests for their own sacrifices. His father had continued to raise the doves as part of his tithes to the Temple, which was a tradition carried on from his ancestors. Those doves were not to be sold by the money-changers and other profiteers, but be given only to the priests.

He had his men deliver the eight carriers with a dozen beautiful doves in each to contact certain priests as his father had instructed them. The servants were told to make contact as soon as they arrived at the Temple. The servants were loyal and obedient, had already carried out his father's orders and had traveled back home.

Aheelim closed his eyes and gave a silent prayer to Yahweh that he had been able to do what he had been instructed. He prayed the animals would be used as directed and their purpose would be fulfilled. He had already sold a portion of his sheep for the various sacrifices, but for the rest he had met with other sheep owners who wanted to purchase rams for breeding to enlarge their own flocks. His father had given him the names and directions to those he should contact, and that business had also been completed.

It had taken a few months to complete his father's business, but now he was able to work on his own agenda. He was happy to then move into the house he was now renting. For a few months he had stayed in various inns in order to carry out that part of his father's business. Inns were noisy and crowded and being in a house by himself was a blessing.

His heart was happy and clear as he walked away from the stock merchant, knowing he did the right thing in turning him down. Humming a jaunty tune, he headed back to the livery to meet with Abner.

Aheelim came through the front, spoke with Abner who quoted Goshen's wages to him, which was more than he believed the man would offer. He was introduced to Pashur, Abner's nephew. The young man seemed to be a bit weak from his bout with illness, but was also handy with the animals.

Abner reported that Goshen was seen to be a hard worker and, he quietly whispered, tended to finish his chores a lot faster than his nephew, which Aheelim was pleased to hear. Being an ex-slave, he knew Goshen's work would be more than acceptable. He would make it a point to stop in every once in a while to see how Goshen was faring in his work.

◆

One day, having nothing else to do, Aheelim went to the livery to check on his horse and mules and Goshen. He stopped first at the table Abner used for his office and conversed with him for a few minutes. When he asked the livery master about Goshen, Abner pointed to an area where hay and grains were kept.

Reaching the hay area, he went to back to meet with the freed slave. Goshen had his mid-day meal on a bale of hay spread out in front of him. Aheelim could see he had his head turned to the side speaking to someone, and upon coming closer saw a pretty young woman sitting on another bale chatting with him. She was possibly 16 or so years, but since she kept her head down, he was unsure.

One thing was noticeable. Goshen had already met a new friend – and female at that!

Goshen turned his head at Aheelim's approach and began to stand, but Aheelim waved his hand, signaling him to remain seated. The young woman turned as he came forward and looked somewhat abashed. She smiled at him and prepared to leave.

"Oh, no, please don't leave on account of me. I just

came to see how my friend was getting along. I'll be leaving in one moment."

Goshen gave a huge grin at his rescuer's use of the word 'friend'. He then stood and made the introduction of the young woman.

"Sir, this is my employer Abner's niece, Tirshah. She did not know I always bring my own mid-day meals and came to give me an extra one she had prepared, along with meals for her uncle and brother, believing I had nothing to eat today. I had already purchased a few food items last night."

The girl smiled as she nodded her head and looked toward the door. Standing at the door were three of the four little girls he had met at the well months ago.

Goshen smiled and gave them a small wave and received three waves in return. Tirshah gave a smile and a small curtsy and in a pretty voice said, "Nice to meet you, sir," and departed.

"I believe she's a little shy," Goshen informed him with a blush. "She's very nice. Those little girls are her nieces. They are Abner's grandchildren by an older daughter."

"Well, you've only been here less than six months and already you're meeting friends. Good for you! I spoke with Abner and he feels you're still doing a good job. I came through the front and noticed Abner's nephew is looking well and back to work full time. He says you're a hard worker. I understand you and his nephew are getting along quite well, which is good and—ah, and with his niece as well, I see."

They chatted for a short while and he told Goshen to finish his meal, knowing the man only had so much time for his midday meal and would soon return to work.

"If you need me, which I'm quite sure you won't, you know where to find me," Aheelim said, as he silently chuckled on his way out.

~32~

Tahmari could not believe dusk was starting to fall. She had stopped by the marketplace to see the merchants' wares and time just seemed to fly. It always amazed her how the Oriental merchants and traders could sell all of their beautiful wares in a day or two, yet she could not find such items in any of the town's Jewish establishments. The silver and gold bracelets, sandals, scarves and pins were marvels.

Many times she would return home and try to duplicate some of their jewelry which looked fine, but not as fine as the ones she had recently seen and touched.

Those traders had the most beautiful materials, but only the wealthy could afford their jewelry, scarves and robes. The soles on their sandals did not quickly wear out, like the ones she had on her own feet. She took the time to touch the laces and note how tightly they were stitched. The beautiful thick coverlets were much heavier than anything she could produce on her loom.

After giving a long sigh, she could see the sun was trying to set and knew it would behoove her to hurry home before dark.

Tahmari soon felt a tingle on the back of her neck. Was she being followed, or was it just her imagination? She heard a soft shuffle as if someone might be following behind her and began to walk more quickly. The steps were heavy so she knew it was a man.

Why did she wait so long to return home? It had been her plan to go to the well and get another vessel of water for the house, but she changed her mind when she saw the traveling merchants heading away from the marketplace. She turned away from their direction and began to walk quickly toward her home.

How foolish! She could have just lingered a few minutes and continued on her way, or she could have just gone earlier in the day to visit the marketplace. Instead she had lingered far too long. The merchants were friendly and had slowed for her to catch up. One thing about the merchants, they didn't mind what type of woman you were—gentlewoman or prostitute—it was their business to make sales, whether during the day or night.

The shuffling was no longer soft, but becoming louder for she could hear the footsteps getting closer. There had been a series of rapes of young women and girls traveling alone and she did not want to be caught. She slipped into a small covered walkway and waited quietly, but by then the footsteps had stopped. Hurriedly, she began a quick walk and then began running. Whoever had been following her must have gone another way because she didn't hear him for a few moments. Suddenly, she heard the steps again and quickened her pace.

Just as she turned the corner, she bumped into a young man approaching her from the opposite direction. He did not see her because he had his head down while doing some figuring on a small piece of parchment, causing him to run into her. He spread his legs to gain balance and grabbed her elbow to keep her from falling backwards. His clothes looked and felt rich, and she realized he was a man of some substance.

Since Tahmari pretty much knew the faces of most of the men in town, it was obvious he was not from the area.

"So-so sorry. Please for-forgive me," she stammered. She cast her eyes behind her as she tried to see if anyone was there.

"Excuse me, miss," said the man's deep voice. "I was rushing and did not look where I was going."

"Quite all right—I-I'm afraid I was not watching either. I'm so sorry."

Tahmari chanced to look behind her and saw the back of the man she presumed had followed her. She could not make out the man's identity for he had turned his face before hurriedly walking away in the opposite direction.

The stranger continued to hold her elbow as he followed her eye movement and observed a man quickly walking away. He could see her fright. Was that man following her? No one else was in the area and all he noticed was a small mongrel ambling a bit behind the woman.

Aheelim observed the makeup on her face and only her eyes showed above her veil, but he could see that she was young and beautiful. As he stared into her eyes, he recognized fear. After all, had he not seen the same sort of fear months ago in the eyes of Goshen?

Self-conscious now, Tahmari discreetly pulled away from the man's hand on her elbow.

"You look pale, young lady. May I be of some help?" The very nice man seemed concerned. "Would you like me to escort you home?"

"Oh, no, no. No, sir. I'm-I'm fine." She hurried from his presence and after taking a hurried look behind her, she began to run. Following close behind ran the little dog.

Once she reached her home, Tahmari leaned against the inside beam, breathing heavily.

She did not doubt someone was following her. She silently gave thanks to Yahweh for her safe return and breathed a huge sigh of relief. She determined to not let time slip away from her again. Many disastrous things took place in the dark and she knew it was wise to only venture out in late day, as opposed to wandering around town at dusk or nightfall.

Who was following her? She did not recognize the man for he had turned his back before she could get a look at his face. And yet, as she thought back, there was something familiar about his back, but knew he was not one of her customers. She could not put her finger on it, but knew she had seen him before.

Shaking off her fear, Tahmari began preparing herself for the evening. It was getting late and she knew she would have someone at her door during the next hour or so and did not have time to waste.

~33~

Her curtain had been pulled over the door to denote there would be no business today for it was the Sabbath and like every good Jew, today was her day of rest. She knew that true Jews would not be coming to her small home today, but the other prostitutes, pagan or otherwise, might be busy with their out-of-town travelers. She was glad she didn't have to bother with travelers because she was not the one to fulfill their unusual sexual requests. Arbor had cautioned her to only service Jewish clients and be specific as to what type of service she would render.

She had cooked her meal the day before for there would be no cooking, cleaning or servicing the needy and greedy men of the town.

She took her small board to the rear of the house and sat on a low stool. Pulling out her small knife, she began to aim for the target as Uncle Josiah had taught her and her friends. As his eyesight began to fail, she found she could win the game of "target" for her aim had greatly improved. She had become almost as good as her friend Mogdi.

Watching the knife fly through the air toward the board, she began to cry. Playing the game always made her feel as if Uncle Josiah was sitting beside her, throwing his knife and laughing when he missed and she didn't. In the beginning she felt he allowed her to win, but over the years she became more practiced.

It had been a long time since she'd brought the board out. Although she cried as she reminisced, it felt good to think of her uncle. Was he in heaven watching her? Was he able to see what her life had become? Would he forgive her for what she now did for a living? Would he still think she was a beautiful young girl, or a heavily-made up prostitute?

When she washed clothes and viewed herself in the river, she never saw the young girl she used to see. There were bags under her eyes; there was no longer a bright gleam to her hair for lately it hung in a limp braid over her shoulder, acknowledging her constant fatigue. Over and over she threw the knife at the board, never missing the center target.

◆

The days were getting shorter and the nights much longer. Giving a huge sigh, she unstuck the knife, picked up the board, and headed back inside the house. As she passed her eating area, she laid the knife on the table and went toward her sleeping pallet. Slowly she began pulling night clothes out of the trunk her uncle had given her to prepare for a quick nap before fixing her evening meal. As she returned the target board against the wall, she heard movement in her front room.

With a frown, she thought to herself: "Didn't the man see the curtain pulled?"

There would be no business today, not on her Sabbath. She may not be a practicing Jew, but she still observed the holy days as she had been taught. She did not undress, but slowly headed toward the front.

Upon reaching the curtain, she could see Teheran weaving back and forth in the doorway with Eliah standing to the side. Because of his stature, she almost didn't see the quiet man with Teheran. She held the curtain back with her left hand as she gestured with her right.

Quietly apologizing, she gave a short nod. "I am sorry, gentlemen, but I am not working today, for as you know today is the Sabbath."

"Izzat so? Izzn't that strange, Eliah—a prostitute who celebrates our holy day?" slurred Teheran.

He was so drunk he was holding onto the side of the doorpost and she believed if he took his hand away, he would fall to the floor. Eliah was not inebriated and had the grace to look a bit embarrassed by his friend's actions.

"We're sorry miss," Eliah said as he kept his eyes on the floor. She could tell he was embarrassed by his friend's drunken antics.

"The other women were busy and he decided we should see if you might be available."

"Thank you, Eliah, but I honor the Sabbath and am closed for the day, however, I will be open tomorrow. Hopefully you can both wait until then."

Eliah looked as if he was about to turn away, but Teheran did not move. Tahmari could see the taller man was becoming angrier in his drunken state. The back of her mind told her that not all of the prostitutes were so busy they could not service one or two more clients. Plus, many do not get a lot of business from the Jews on the holy days, most certainly not the Sabbath, and since most of the prostitutes do not celebrate the occasion, not a lot of money is generated.

The women probably refused Teheran because of his drunkenness. Even a good wife would stay out the way of her husband if he was drunk.

She had been told there were people who understood the meaning of a closed curtain as a "no" for receiving any type of service. Even the non-Jewish shopkeepers, knowing the Jews did not work or purchase any products on the holy days used it as their day of rest. The ones on the traveling carts were known to place a tent-like material across the tops of their wares.

There were also pagan traders who knew that a closed curtain on the Jewish Sabbath meant they would make very few sales. She also knew of two other Jewish prostitutes besides herself and one of them was also known to refuse to work on the Jewish holy days.

Teheran quickly moved his hand toward her as if to grab her arm, but she was much quicker and backed far enough away from him. She could smell his sour sweat, which was also similar to urine. Although his clothes seemed clean, his breath and body odor was not.

"If you were really Jewish you wouldn't be looking for a prostitute at all. You would be killed, you know. The Law says so and I'm quite sure you know that!" Teheran almost shouted the words at her.

Tahmari became angry and loudly retorted, "And if you were a TRUE JEW, you wouldn't be drunk, weaving in my doorway or going from prostitute house to prostitute house looking for someone to service you! Especially with today being the Sabbath!"

She could see Teheran was angry as well as drunk, and that Eliah was showing signs of unease. The quiet man was shifting from one foot to the other. There was an apology in his eyes as he began grabbing at Teheran's robe trying to pull him from the doorway, but his friend gave him a belligerent look before shaking him off.

His enraged voice became a loud drunken snarl. "You female cur—you're no better than the rest of those prostitutes and yet you try to put on airs. Is this because you claim to be Jewish? 'Service,' service you say? Is that the word you use instead of saying what you really do? 'Service,' bah! Another word for what you women do with the men and what the men do to you. Just because you live on this side of town makes no difference to me! I'm quite sure that even the priests come over here to get what they want!"

With one hand on her hip, she wagged her finger in his face.

"For your information, no priest has ever come to my door, and furthermore, even if they did require my services, they certainly wouldn't show up on the Sabbath, drunk with cheap wine. Get away from my house, Teheran, and when you sober up, don't you even think about coming back!"

He moved toward her again, but he was so drunk his lack of speed and direction caused his arm to catch the side of the curtain, causing it to wrap around his hand. Teheran struggled to release his sleeve from the curtain.

Eliah was trying very hard to cajole him into leaving, which he refused to do. By now, Tahmari was fearful and started toward her back room where there was another opening, but the drunkard followed hurriedly behind her – gutturally snarling. In the back of her mind, she thought she heard the little dog outside her home snarling and barking.

She knew she might have to get away from the house quickly and at the same time, the thought came to her what Dorit had told her.

"Always keep a sharp weapon somewhere near that you can reach in the event there is a problem." She never thought she would have to keep a weapon in her own home, nor that it would be her little knife.

Tahmari flew to the side room with him on her heels as she headed toward the table, immediately grabbing the small knife by the handle. Turning, she angrily slashed three times at his light-colored robe, leaving three long stains which quickly spread across the expensive material.

Caught by surprise, Teheran looked down at the stains and, as his eyes widened, quickly backed away. She watched his eyebrows shoot upward to the top of his forehead. Stupefied, he was now beginning to sober.

At that moment, Eliah reached out and pulled back the loose material of his friend's robe and both quickly turned and ran toward the front of the house. Tahmari watched as the curtain slowly swayed and returned to its original hanging position.

Breathing heavily, Tahmari quickly closed her small door. She went to the window and watched as the two men hurried around the next building with the small dog running behind, yipping at their heels. She gave a nervous laugh at the scene as she felt relief at their leaving.

She realized that during the time she slashed his robe, she really wanted to kill the man. If it was not for the loose robe covering his chest, she would have done so.

"Oh, my sovereign God!" she moaned as she slowly sat on the small stool beside the window, covering her face with her hands and rocked from side to side.

"It's bad enough that things were out of hand, but I believe I wanted to kill him. He was insufferable. Please Lord, forgive me. Thank you for not allowing me to kill him."

She began to silently sob as she thought about what had just taken place. As the tears flowed down her cheeks, she could only think of Uncle Josiah putting his hand on her head and telling her what a good niece she was.

You shall not kill—she knew the Commandment—but what about 'you shall not think about killing'?

She had never had any relations or interactions with Teheran. Her one time with Eliah was for less than twenty minutes, sitting and talking quietly about the town and the Temple, and he then went on his way. She knew he only came for conversation, but he was known as a friend and follower of Teheran. On that one day, however, he was alone and possibly lonely.

She had the impression he only came to her small home because he had nowhere else to go, and since he was on her side of town, he decided to visit her. He also paid her more than what was necessary although they had no intimacy, for which she was grateful.

Thinking back, she began to believe it was Teheran who followed her the other night. She could not actually be sure, but his height and his stance made her think it was so. She was happy the stranger had come along when he did.

On the days following, whenever Teheran would see her, he would scowl, but not say anything to her. The man was not married, and if he had any family, she did not know. She believed he and Eliah got along because the little man liked being seen in his company and Teheran enjoyed having a follower.

Yet, she had the feeling that Eliah had just seen another side to his friend that he had never seen before, and the scowl on his face showed he did not like it.

~34~

She was standing at a trader's wagon looking at the earrings, beads, and stones. She kept an eye on the time of day, for she did not want to again be caught off guard by traveling home in late evening. She began fingering a beautiful scarf she knew she could not afford, but in her mind, she envisioned her own trader's cart.

She had begun making small jeweled bangles and rings and wanted to become proficient in jewelry-making so that when she was ready to become a merchant, she would have wares to sell. This merchant had purchased a few of her jeweled bracelets, scarves and script bags and smiled as she perused his merchandise.

She picked up one of the beautiful scarves and smelled the perfume emanating from the material, suddenly becoming aware of a small man standing beside her and touching her elbow.

Tahmari was surprised and stared at the man for she had never seen him before. He did not look menacing, but stood close and put his hand on her arm. Leaning toward her he whispered softly in her ear.

"Luchi asked that I find you and tell you to go to Dorit's house now. It is very important."

After placing the scarf back on its shelf, she turned to thank the man for his message, and found he had disappeared. Quickly, she headed toward Dorit's house.

Something must be wrong, she thought, for Luchi had never sent her a message before. She was very quiet and always let Kiri and Garner speak for her. Of the three women, she seldom gave an opinion.

As Tahmari came around the side of Dorit's house, she was surprised to see another black man standing with Arbor in front. The visitor stood, stepped forward, and bowed low. She was not aware that Arbor had a brother or any other relative.

"Good day, miss," he said in a dialect similar to Arbor's. He was not quite as tall and slightly lighter in complexion, but had presence. His beard was short and his head was full of small braids which fell across his shoulder. His robe was a light weave and it seemed to her that Arbor had been crying.

Her heart skipped a beat.

Understanding his sorrow, she shook her head and began to moan, "Oh, no, oh, no."

Looking past the men, she saw a room full of prostitutes in Dorit's sitting room. Some were sitting and others were standing and all looked as if they had been crying. Incense was burning and there was food and fruit on the hall table. On the side were small jugs, presumably filled with wine and water. She watched as Luchi came toward her and put her arms around her.

"Yes, my dear. Dorit has gone to a better place. She'll have no more pain or sorrow. She always considered herself Jewish, but because of what she was, there will not be a priest to say a few words over her body. We were waiting for you. Is there a prayer you Jews use that would be appropriate to say over her body? We will be taking her to an area that has been set aside for her burial. Arbor and Najur will help us."

"Najur? Is that the man outside with Arbor? Have I seen him before?"

"Probably not, but every few months he comes to town and always pays a visit with Arbor and Dorit," Garner answered.

"In his country, he is considered a priest of some sort. He and Arbor have been friends for a long time, but he's been traveling with his master and has just now returned to the town. He's a eunuch also, but has a lot of freedom."

"Najur calls his god 'Creator' but to me this god sounds like your God. According to him, you can't see him or touch his God, so his god sounds like yours. He will help in presiding over Dorit's burial."

"Dorit used to put a lot of confidence in this man whenever he would come back to town and they would talk about their God. All of us know that when you would visit her, the two of you would discuss your God, and she loved the fact that you were schooled in the Hebrew history and language. Since we all have different beliefs and you were Jewish, she enjoyed your visits all the more."

◆

Tahmari entered the house and the women looked sorrowfully at her as Kiri and a few others led her to Dorit's body. Since the weather was so warm and Dorit had been ill for some time, she knew the burial would take place right away or the body would begin to smell. Dorit always had an odd odor and now she could smell a sweet, heady scent.

She knew Arbor had bathed the body with special oils and the ointment which he used to keep the insects away. There were linen strips situated under the body, and other strips hanging off the table that would be used to wrap her for burial.

A few more women came into the small room. Silently joining hands, they made a circle around the body. Tahmari bowed her head and the others did the same. She was not sure what to say for she was in a room full of women who were, as far as she knew, pagan prostitutes.

Closing her eyes, she said, "Bless her soul, Yahweh, for she taught us to worship You, the unseen God, and to remain in faith through her love for You. Our prayers are for her as her body goes back to dust and her soul into your hands. We know Dorit believed in the resurrection and it is our hope that she will participate in it. Although unable to be a practicing Jew, but still a woman who was created by You, we gather here to say our last goodbye. We all thank you for letting us know her and feel the warmth of her presence as friend to us all. Selah and amen."

By this time, Arbor and Najur had come into the room and the women made room for them to link their hands. Bowing his head, Najur recited a prayer in an unknown language, but Tahmari caught the words 'Yahweh' and 'Elohim' and when he finished, she quickly looked at him. Upon the prayer's end, he looked at her. Their eyes locked and nodding, smiled at each other.

A few of the prostitutes mumbled prayers to their gods. Following the prayers, as one the women bent toward the table, picked up the strips and edges of the linen material and slowly began wrapping the body. Within minutes the body was tightly wrapped and left on the slab of wood. Immediately the women began to wail and cry, hugging one another. This lasted for a few minutes as the women mourned for their beloved friend.

Arbor stood at the head and Najur stood at the feet as the women lined up on both sides of the body. A rustling noise was heard outside the door and breathing heavily, Turza entered the room and went toward the men who sat the slab of wood down for a few minutes and whispered.

"It is ready, and thank you," Turza spoke to Najur.

He had placed himself between Najur and Arbor and whispered to them a bit more information. Going back to the front and rear of the slab, Arbor and Najur nodded to the women.

Dorit was so small that her body seemed to be lightweight. Ten women, including Tahmari, positioned themselves, five on each side of the slab. The women lifted the wood and began following the three men, who led the way to the burial site. Behind them came more women with flowers and small trinkets in their hands. Tahmari believed the linen cloths weighed more than the body, which had begun to stiffen as there was a slight bounce on the wood she was lying on.

Turning her head, she noticed following behind the women the small dog who had his head down. She believed she heard him whimpering. Strange, it was almost as if he also mourned.

They carried Dorit to a deserted area behind a row of houses where a hole was ready for her body to be deposited. Najur and Arbor smiled at Turza, who nodded his head. It was at that time she realized Turza had procured Dorit's resting place and the money for it was probably donated by the eunuchs.

Garner pressed a few flowers into Tahmari's hands and hugged her. One by one, flowers and trinkets were dropped by the women into the hole, then the body.

Tahmari was the last to place her flowers on top. Once again the women began to wail and cry.

Not knowing what was required of her, Tahmari stood with the wailing women beside the small grave as the men threw dirt on top and closed it. Only the three men and the prostitutes attended the short ceremony, yet Tahmari saw standing a little ways to the side the little man who delivered Luchi's message, and a small group of older men. She knew the others also saw them, but no one uttered a word.

The last item to go into the hole was a beautiful bracelet that Tahmari could see looked familiar. She believed it to be similar, if not the same style of bracelet she had been given by Uncle Josiah. Arbor slowly knelt to place it lovingly into the grave when she noticed it was exactly like hers. It seemed odd to see two bracelets looking so much alike.

As she caught her breath, she saw Arbor slightly turn his head to look toward her. She looked questioningly at him, but he had turned his head to continue shoveling the dirt into the hole.

The women turned as one and headed back to Dorit's house. Arbor and Najur had prepared a simple meal for the women. At first it was quiet, and then one by one the women began to reminisce with tidbits about Dorit. They remembered advice she had given them, some jokes she told, and how each came to know her. Tahmari was surprised to learn that their stories were similar to hers for most of the women also had no male protection.

Arbor announced that none of Dorit's clothes would be given away, for he would be burning them, but any memento they wished to have from the house they should take it now. This was Dorit's request.

Tahmari took a set of Dorit's small Jewish candlesticks holders and candles. As the others began to pick up small pottery items, she turned to Arbor.

"What will you do now, Arbor? Will you remain here? You know you are welcome to stay with any of us. My house is small but I would be happy to have you live with me."

"No, my dear, but thank you. I will be leaving with Najur and will be working with Najur's master's brother who lives a few days walk from here. He wants me to be his valet and I will have a new home. I will do for him what I did for my old master and for Dorit. I have already packed and will leave in the morning.

One nice thing is that I will not be a slave, but a servant, and will receive wages for my services. Plus, while living here, Dorit set aside money for my services, and whenever I took care of the ladies, their friends, and people who needed doctoring, they would give me money. I never went into my savings for I had need of nothing. Dorit took care of the bills and purchases for the house."

As they began to leave, Arbor turned to the women

and held his arms out to each one. He was trying very hard not to cry in front of them, but as they began crying on his chest, he broke down and sobbed. They all wished him well and slowly left the house.

Najur told them the house had been sold over a year ago by Dorit. She had made a deal with the new owner, a wealthy Jewish businessman and friend of his master, to be allowed to live there until she died. He would soon be sending servants to come and ready the house for the man's invalid stepson. Since the house was not in the same neighborhood of the prostitutes, the son would still be able to live in peace with his nurse.

Each of the women was given a small packet of food from the gathering after the burial. When the women reached their respective homes, they noticed a small bag with money inside. It was Dorit's wish that each of her friends receive money to cover a few days of not working should they wish to mourn her passing.

Tahmari was one of the last to hug Arbor and he asked that she wait just a moment for the others to leave. Tahmari was not sure what he wanted to say, but she waited. He and Najur stood beside the door and continued their goodbyes to the women.

~35~

Arbor then turned to her and quietly began to explain about the bracelet.

"Years ago, before I came to serve Dorit, there was an argument between Dorit and a very wealthy businessman who was one of Jerusalem's officials and one of this town's top leaders. He's dead now. He used her and other prostitutes brutally and refused to pay. The women went before the town's magistrate who did not want to hear their case because of what the women did for a living. He wouldn't even bring out the black and white stones for the verdict. He just refused to hear the case.

The ladies felt even if he didn't pronounce the stones, he could have at least heard their side of the story, but he refused."

"The stones? What about the stones?" she asked.

"If guilty, the black stone would have been placed on the stand, and if not guilty, the white stone. I believe it is how many Jewish cases are conducted."

"But it seems the official had previously done this to a few other prostitutes who did not pursue any action because of his status, for they felt why try? The women knew they could not win the case because of who the man was and their occupation."

"But Dorit suggested they all band together as one and try again. Although they were in their rights, the magistrate was a friend to the official, so he refused to hear their case."

"Your Uncle Josiah met them outside of the courts and, after hearing their problem, became their advocate. The next day he went before the same magistrate and pleaded their case. He mentioned if he did not do right by the prostitutes, news of it could reach the Temple priests, the townspeople, the wealthy man's family, as well as the Sanhedrin. After all, the man had status and one thing he did not want to lose was his status in society."

"To remain powerful in Jerusalem, the Temple and the town, your uncle made the suggestion it would be best for the magistrate to hear the case secretly, have the official pay the women what they were owed and more, with the suggestion there be a condition where the women would keep the matter quiet if paid. Otherwise he, himself, would make sure it was known what the man had been doing with the prostitutes and how he was negligent in paying what was owed."

"Within days, the magistrate spoke with the official and all of the ladies were paid as promised, as well as given an amount for them to keep quiet about the entire affair. Your uncle refused their offer of payment and suggested they be more careful in entertaining clients such as that man." Arbor gave a slight chuckle at the remark.

"Since he would not take payment for his help, instead the ladies all purchased special items for him and his wife, who was alive at that time—scarves, sandals, chalices, and even a few Jewish artifacts and put the presents beside his door. That way he could not turn down their gifts."

"When she heard Josiah was raising his little niece, Dorit later took some of her money, went to a silversmith and had three silver and jeweled bracelets made in the same design. She gave your uncle one of the bracelets for his wife, one for his niece, and the last she kept for herself."

"As her illness progressed, she made plans for many of her personal items. One of the last items she gave me before she passed away was the bracelet. She wanted me to place it in her grave when she died. She told me the story and made me promise to hold it until this day."

"She used to say, 'I really don't know where I would wear it.' I knew you would recognize it because of its design and because you once tried to sell yours to pay your uncle's doctors' fees. After your uncle died, you couldn't get a buyer to pay you what you felt it was worth, so I knew you still have it."

"I was in the shop when you tried to barter with the merchant and recognized the bracelet as the same one I had in safekeeping for Dorit. When I placed it in her grave, I knew you would recognize it." Arbor gave a broad smile.

"Yes, Dorit realized you were Josiah's niece when you first came to her. She had not seen you since you were very young. That is why she did not want you to become a prostitute and took so long to give you an answer. She wanted you to be very sure because she knew your uncle did not raise you to be a harlot."

Tahmari's eyes watered. "Yes, Arbor, I still have the other bracelet. It was given to me by Uncle Josiah to wear on special occasions. He told me it was worth quite a bit and also had sentimental value, which is why I knew I could get more than what was offered. Thank you so much for telling me."

"I had heard that my uncle once helped some prostitutes, but never knew the story. Even one of the Temple guards once told me my uncle was helpful to others as well as those who could not speak for themselves."

She blinked quickly to keep her tears from falling. "I never knew Dorit was one of those he helped. Again, thank you for telling me."

Reaching up she grabbed the eunuch, gave him a huge hug and kissed him noisily on his cheek, mingling her tears with his.

"Be well, Arbor, and enjoy the new journey you will be traveling. I pray Yahweh blesses you richly in your new position."

As she headed for home, she looked in her bag and saw that Arbor had placed enough food to last her a couple of days, as well as coins that were worth the amount of a week's work.

Hugging the bag to her chest, she continued walking with tears coursing down her cheeks.

Tahmari again noticed the small dog which she had been seeing more often lately following behind her. She then sat sadly by the side of the road, giving the dog bits and pieces of her food. As the dog chewed, his eyes looked up at the crying woman who had been feeding him and began to whine.

~36~

The month after Dorit's passing was uneventful. To break the monotony, Tahmari decided to head toward Garner's house to visit and was surprised to see her packing furniture and other items into a small wagon. It did not take her long to realize her friend was in the process of moving. Quickening her steps, she stood between her friend and the wagon.

"Garner, are you all right? Why are you packing? Are you moving?"

Garner was dressed in a beautiful scarf which draped over her shoulders, covering her top. Her face was haggard and it looked as if she had been crying. She turned and gave her friend a hug.

"Oh, Tahmari! I was going to come see you before I left, but it is imperative that I leave right away. Things have been happening to me and my property this past month. Yesterday, while I was away, someone broke into my home and vandalized it, breaking pottery and writing filthy words on my walls. A few days ago, my religious statues disappeared and some of my clothes were ripped. It did not take me long to realize someone poured salt over my garden, for the plants and vegetables that were alive are now dead. They were thriving a few weeks ago and they slowly became withered or dead. Something is going on and I am becoming fearful that harm will eventually come to me."

"It is no use going to the magistrates because they refuse to help prostitutes with our legal problems. Besides, I don't know who is doing these acts of vandalism. These occurrences have made me deathly afraid so I'm moving. My regular customers have dwindled down to very few. Because of that and other happenings, I have had very uneasy feelings these past few weeks. I have a few friends who live in small dwellings near the hillside and I once lived with one of them for a few days. It was then I realized it was time to move on."

"Like you, Garner, I also feel as if something is going on and there seems to be unrest in the air. I will pray for your safety and will only say, go with Yahweh, Garner." Tahmari sighed and gave her a quick hug.

"Thank you, my friend. Since I met Dorit and have known you, I also thank you for the strength and faith you both have in your God. I have never put much faith in the gods I was raised with, and frankly do not worship any god, but I was beginning to believe in Dorit's God. But yes, do pray for me."

"Where are you going? Do you have a destination?"

"No, I have no destination, but I'll know when I get there. I want you to know that I will miss you so much."

Garner hugged her again as she hesitantly said, "And may your God be with you also."

Garner kissed Tahmari's forehead, picked up a small bag and deposited it on the wagon's seat as she climbed inside. Picking up the reins to her mule, she gave a little clicking sound with her tongue and slowly moved down the road toward the outskirts of town.

As Tahmari headed for her home, she hesitated, turned right and headed toward Luchi's home.

She found Luchi in the rear of her small home checking out her garden. When she heard steps behind her she turned and smiled at Tahmari.

"Good to see you, my friend. I supposed you were on this side of town to visit with Garner. Did she tell you she was leaving the area?" Her eyes were sad as she stepped around her small garden.

"Luchi," she started, "did you know about the troubles Garner had been experiencing lately? When she told me about the break in at her house and the many problems that have taken place lately, I was surprised."

"I did not know all of it, but she told me some things yesterday evening when I went to see her. I never thought about checking my garden. My small crop looks good and is still thriving, thank the gods."

.. "Garner was already packed this morning, and had

purchased a wagon and an animal to hitch to it. At first I was surprised, but when I visited another prostitute, she told me that some of the men she used to regularly have as clients have stopped coming to her house and she wondered if someone had put out a rumor about us. When I asked why, she said she did not know, but one of her clients suggested she put away her religious statues. She said she wondered about that, but did so."

"Why are you looking at your garden? Your crops look well. I never knew you had a small olive tree back here. In fact, this is the first time I've ever been behind your house."

Tahmari continued to be amazed at how well the gardens grew on this side of town, better than behind her house. Of course, when Uncle Josiah was alive, he cultivated the garden and they always had enough vegetables for their meals and purchased only olives and fruits from the merchants when they came by.

Luchi's brows came together as she looked up.

"After Garner told me how someone poured salt on the soil around her plants, I've been watching mine. No one has touched my garden, but there is a sense of unease among the prostitutes in the city. I don't plan to move like Garner, but even I am being more cautious lately. I also removed my religious statues from near the front of my house. Most of my regulars still visit me, but not on their usual days and times."

"Before on various days, I always knew who to expect at certain times, but some are arriving at my door on irregular days, and one time two came at the same time and I had to inform them I never do two clients at once. I may be a prostitute, but I do have my standards. That's one thing I learned from Dorit."

Luchi gave a long sigh and looked sad.

"Be careful, Tahmari. All I can say is be very careful and watch for signs of unrest."

Nodding her agreement, Tahmari hugged her and took her leave.

Nothing out of the ordinary took place the rest of the week. Things seemed to go back to normal and the prostitutes continued their business without any mishaps.

~37~

One of her older and more friendly clients began discussing current news he'd heard around the town. Sometimes he would come to have her read his letters or chatter about the latest news in the area. Generally Tahmari enjoyed catching up on such items, but today her mind had wandered and she vaguely listened because he had a tendency to ramble on.

At one point he mentioned the name 'Meka' and at this her hearing perked up. He was girding his script belt across his robe and had his head down as he picked up the notes he had previously allowed her to read.

Right away he segued into talking about his youngest daughter and how happy he was that her husband enjoyed reading his letters to her, for she was not educated. Still rambling, he announced his grandson would soon be three years old.

"My daughter is always happy to receive letters from me. Thank you, my dear. I know my daughter figured out that I was not the writer of the notes, and I appreciate everything you do for me. Just so you know I put a little extra money in your pouch."

Tahmari turned and looked at him. "Meka? Did you say, 'Meka'? Meka, who used to live here but moved with her family a few years back?"

"Yes, did you know her?" At her sad nod, his face fell.

"I am sorry to say she passed away. She came for a visit, became very ill and died last week. Her daughter said it was her wish to be buried here. I'm sorry she passed away but was glad she was already here and did not have to have her body travel from wherever she was living. I hate to be the bearer of bad news, my dear, for I can see you thought kindly of her."

Tahmari did not say anything, but put the payment pouch on the small table, wished him well and thanked him for telling her about Meka's passing.

After he left, she began to silently cry. Her one true friend from her youth was Meka, and now she was dead. Although Meka had moved far away, she still thought about her friend and her family and prayed for them. She once had other friends, but they were no longer in contact with her.

Everyone she dearly loved was now dead or gone — her parents, her aunt and uncle, Dorit, and now Meka. She also truly missed her friends, Arbor and Garner. She was so sad she finally got up from the bed, pulled the curtain across her door, went back to her bed and lay across it.

After a few hours, she slowly arose, and began clearing her bed in preparation for the next day.

~38~

It was not necessary for her to walk in the direction of Garner's former house that afternoon, but something drew her to the area. She had only been there a few times before and each time it was toward the end of the day. Months had passed, and as she approached the house, an older woman stood outside the door. Her veil noted that she was also a prostitute.

Of course, it did not matter, for the old house was in the harlot district. Garner once told her she bought the shanty from a prostitute who died from a disease about six months previous to purchasing it. Generally, the unknown disease of a prostitute was always sexual in nature.

Garner had used a few of her clients to help repair some of the outer wood and stone that was falling off, and kept her walkway clear of debris. Her house became one of the better looking ones after she purchased it. For the men's help, she gave them free 'service' in return. The house now looked as if it was again in disrepair and the walkway was not clear.

Tahmari always made sure her home was presentable — not only for her customers, but because that was the way she normally kept it when Uncle Josiah was alive. Of course, she had sold off some of her furnishings in order to pay her uncle's doctor bills, so it was easy to keep in good order.

Turning aside, she saw the same little dog sitting beside the house next to Garner's. Could that be where the dog lived? She never really thought about the dog having an owner since it seemed to roam the entire area and showed up in the most unusual places.

The dog must have been running very hard for she could see it was breathing heavily with his tongue hanging out, and appeared exhausted. He began to whine as he lay down, as if he could run no further.

Suddenly, a much larger dog came running from the back of the house and headed directly for the smaller dog. The little dog was so tired it could hardly stand and the fear in its eyes unnerved her. The larger dog was running fast, hunched over and snarling as it quickly approached.

As if on reflex, she picked up some stones and began throwing them at the dog. One of the larger stones hit the dog on the back leg, which caused it to stop in its tracks. Knowing she had the advantage, she picked up more stones and began hurtling them as fast as she could, a few hitting it in the side. The little dog sat on its haunches and just watched while slowly wagging its tail.

As the big dog began yelping loudly in pain, it turned and ran in the opposite direction. The little one came nearer to her, but not too close. He tried to stand and turned his head to the side. She could see he was breathing heavily as he studied her intently.

"Are you okay? Was that big dog bothering you?" Suddenly she began to laugh and thought to herself: Here I am asking an animal a question and it cannot give me an answer one way or the other. The little dog looked as if he was smiling at her and gave a tired bark as it finally stood.

Once again, she began walking toward home and the dog followed her. How odd, she thought. Whenever I needed solace this little dog has always been nearby. I'm glad I was able to be of help to him. Hmmm. Perhaps we were put on this earth to take care of each other. Everyone needs someone she thought as she smiled.

Turning from the street, she headed back to her side of town. Right away she noticed the dog, although small, was an adult male and was following at a distance behind her. Because he was a small dog, his size made him look young, and she could see he was older than she thought.

Hmm, I wonder who really owns him? She knew there were very few dogs in the area. Most of the townspeople could barely afford food for themselves or their families, let alone a pet dog.

~39~

Time flowed from one week to the next, then into the next year. Although her time of grief for Dorit and Meka had ended, she still thought fondly of both and of her friends, Arbor and Garner. Even Najur, whom she barely knew, would come to mind. Her attitude was a happy one, and people were still smiling as the Feast of Esther and the Days of Purim came to a close.

Hurrying, Tahmari decided to take a short cut to her home. It was past the time she would normally go to retrieve water from the town's well and she wanted to be home before the sun actually set.

Carrying her heavy water pot, she thought she heard a sound similar to a cat's cry. She ignored the sound at first, but when it sounded again from the nearby alley, she slowly backed up. There had been news of rapes in the area and she did not want to become a victim.

As she rounded the corner of a building, she saw a slight movement. For safety reasons, she was not sure whether to hurry on or check it out. She hesitated, but took a quick peek and saw the figure of a female with her back against the building, half lying and half sitting on the ground. It was nearing dusk, but she recognized a girl somewhat younger than herself who looked to be in distress.

Tahmari quickly put her water pot on the ground and ran toward her. Kneeling down she put her arms around the girl's waist and back and tried to lift her to a sitting position, quickly noticing the stomach bulge. The girl looked at her in fear and scrambled as she tried to sit up, but Tahmari helped her lay back down so that she would not be in more pain.

Giving a loud moan and breathing heavily, the girl hesitantly said, "I believe I am going into labor for the baby is trying to come. My water burst, but I don't know what to do and I'm scared. Ah, oohh!"

Putting her hands on her stomach, she stuttered as she sobbed, "I j-just don't know what to do!"

'Where do you live? Is there someone I can get for you? Your husband or mother?"

"I have no husband and my family doesn't want me. I came here to die. My family has been shamed by me and ... oh, ooohhh! I don't know what to do-o-o!"

The girl continued to sob and her moans became louder as the contractions came closer.

Tahmari knew she also was not sure what to do. She had once attended a birthing some years ago with her friend and housekeeper, Meka, but all she did was run errands to make sure there was a lot of straw, cloths, swaddling material and hot water available as the midwives requested.

Turning her head, she heard the slight rumbling of a trader's or merchant's wagon slowly moving toward the alley.

"I'll be right back!" She ran behind the rear of the wagon, yelling for it to stop. The wagon kept rolling, so she began banging her fist on the side, as she continued screaming for help.

The driver, an older man in a festive tarbūsh fez who looked to be handsome but somewhat foreign, began to draw back on the reins of the two mules that were hitched up front, and stared at her. His smooth skin was a light honey color that she found belied his age. She could tell he was older, but not very old. His gray hair was a salt and pepper color showing a few wayward strands peeking out from under his hat and his salt and pepper beard was nicely trimmed.

In halting Aramaic he began his sales pitch, "Is there something you wish to purchase, lady? I have pots, scarves, jewelry, sandals . . .," he started, but noticing her distress he stopped.

Panting from her run, Tahmari stopped beating on the side of the wagon and bent to put her hands on her knees as she took in large gulps of air in order to speak.

"There's a young lady in labor in the alley here and I need your help. Please help us!"

The man turned around to part the curtain in the wagon and shouted something in another language where two adult women stuck their heads out. A younger woman stuck her head between them through the curtains and hesitantly asked what she wanted. She spoke first in another language, then switched to Aramaic. Tahmari breathed a sigh of relief that the younger woman understood her language and explained what she needed. The younger woman then turned and relayed her message to the older women on each side of her.

The two older women quickly girded their clothing, jumped from the wagon, then followed behind Tahmari while using their hands to chatter to each other in a foreign language as they ran toward the alley.

They reached the pregnant girl, and after kneeling and lifting the girl's skirt, one put both hands to the sides of her face, whispered something to the other and both gave 'tch, tch' sounds. They talked among themselves for a few seconds and in broken Aramaic the older woman turned and shouted to Tahmari:

"Where your house? We need house! Baby want to come now!'

She shouted something to the younger one in the wagon, who quickly began moving things around. Half lifting the girl by feet and shoulders, the three women and the man helped to lift the sobbing girl into the back section.

Not knowing what else to do, Tahmari picked up her water pot and spoke to the younger woman, suggesting they follow her toward her house which was not very far.

The man gave a command to his mules, expertly turned the wagon around and followed her. Although it was only a few minutes, it seemed as if hours had passed by the time they reached her house. The man parked his wagon in front of the door and all four helped to get the moaning girl inside. Tahmari hurriedly fixed a pallet, placing pillows, covered straw and an old curtain under the pregnant woman. She found a few towels and began to heat the water as the younger woman brought more towels and cloths from the wagon.

To make sure no one would come by, she pulled the curtain across the front door indicating she was closed for the evening.

Waving his hands and shooing her aside, the man said something to her which she understood to mean the women would take care of everything. He then stood, leaning against the house and waited. Within a few minutes, the youngest woman came out, retrieved a few more cloths, and ran back inside. Unrolling a blanket, Tahmari placed several hands full of straw on it and the man took it inside.

It was not long before one of the women shouted for the man, who ran to the door and answered some questions. She watched as he went to the rear of her house, found her store of kindling and carried an armful into the house to start a fire in the brazier.

Out of the corner of his eye, the man noticed a small dog lying to the right of Tahmari's kindling. The dog lifted his head and stood after a short while, shook himself as if he was wet, then went to the far side of the house where he again laid down with his head on his front paws. For a few seconds, dog and man stared at each other and after a few moments, the man headed back into the house as the dog ambled away.

Strange! He seldom saw dogs in this town, but looking at the observant dog was not his affair. The dog did not growl at him or bark. Hmm, friendly, he thought. Perhaps the dog belongs to the pretty lady. Perhaps the dog was her security, for in her profession, she probably needed one.

Completing his task, the man returned to his position to stand beside the door, waiting for an assignment from the women inside.

Not knowing what else to do, Tahmari grabbed a stool and sat outside the door. She began to feel as if she was Arbor. Is this how he felt as he waited for Dorit to awaken? She began wringing her hands and praying for Yahweh to help the girl and her unborn child, and included the family who were working with her. The man had returned to his former position after quietly saying, "soon, soon" then once again became silent.

She had been sitting for some time, perhaps hours she thought, and it was not long until an infant's feeble cry was heard and she breathed a sigh of relief. She didn't realize how strained her nerves were until then.

As the cries became lusty, she began to worry where the baby and its mother could stay—for she did not have quarters in her small house for the girl and her baby. The new mother had mentioned that she had no place to go for she had shamed her family. She also wondered if she should pay the merchant's family for their services. What do midwives make? What happens next? This certainly was not the place for a newborn or its mother.

As these thoughts tumbled inside her head, the man, who had gone back inside, came to the door and beckoned her to come to stand with him at the side of the house.

He explained in halting Aramaic that his family was the Pooka family and that his family has been merchants for more than ten generations. His family is well respected in his area, and known as upstanding. Except for the silk scarves, all of his wares were made by his family, including pots, pans and even sandals.

He, his sister and his wife, as well as his youngest daughter were helping the new mother who was now weak from the birthing ordeal, but doing very well.

His sister is one of the midwives in his village and his wife and daughters have always helped her. The family was from an area she had never heard of north of the Sea of Galilee, but then, too, she had never traveled outside of her own area.

He explained that he and his wife also have a son who is a blacksmith and another daughter, but she was not with them this trip for she was home with her husband.

Taking a deep breath, he pointed to the main room where the mother and infant were situated.

"Daughter made suggestion and we believe it good one. We talk it over. Wife and sister agree. We take mother and baby girl with us, okay? Yelada is mother name. She no want to do anything with this baby. Wife make her nurse baby because baby need milk. She no want baby and no want to name baby because of rape. We take care of her and baby like one of us. She tell daughter she no place to go, but we know she need family around for she still weak."

"Wife, sister and daughter say we will be her family, okay? Is all right with you? We stay with you three days, okay? Then we leave for our home. Okay?"

It did not take Tahmari long to decipher his words and meaning, so she nodded her head to each question. She was not responsible for the girl, but since she was the one to engage their services and everyone was in her house, it was not hard to make that assumption.

So the baby was a girl and, from the sounds she heard, healthy. The mother, Yelada, must be doing well for he did not say otherwise. If the merchant wanted the mother and baby, that would solve her most pressing problem. She understood the Pookas felt they could not take the mother and baby without asking permission. Strange, he never named his wife, sister or daughter. He just called them what they were to him – his wife, his sister and his daughter.

"You're correct. The girl and her baby need a family around. I am so happy for her that you will become her new family."

Unsure of what else to do, she reached inside her robe and pulled out her script bag to find some coins. She seldom let anyone see her bag, for male Jews kept writing materials and traveling money inside and very few knew she could read, write or figure. In fact, those who did happen to notice the bag believed it to have belonged to one of her clients, or a relative who may have given it to her as a gift. Truth in fact, she designed, sewed, and decorated her own bag.

After she pressed the coins into his palm, the man smiled, showing a gap in his very white teeth. He then turned and placed the coins on her small table.

"We no need money. You keep. You good lady. What you do is not good, but we do not judge. Our god give you favor and enrich your life."

Pooka scrutinized her script bag and nodding his head, she believed he approved of her handiwork.

She was surprised by his words realizing he had

figured out her occupation, but nodded her thanks. She did not know which god the family worshipped, but silently gave thanks to Yahweh for His favor to Yelada, the infant, and the Pooka family. The women had been more than generous and hospitable to her. She could think of nothing more she could give them. Their energy and laughter filled her house.

She did not understand their language or all they said to each other, but she could tell there was an abundance of love in that family. When they spoke to each other they used their native language, but when they spoke with her they used Aramaic. She presumed that since they visited so many different areas, they had learned enough of various languages to communicate their wares to potential customers.

~40~

Tahmari kept her curtain closed for three full days. She sometimes sat with the mother while she slept or nursed, but they had very little conversation. While the Pookas were there, the merchant and his family kept watch over the new mother and infant, cooked wonderful meals and kept her small house tidy.

Whenever she tried to cook or do any housework, the women would shoo her away to make sure she sat back down while they performed household tasks, even to retrieving food supplies and water from the well in town. The husband made sure there was more than adequate kindling in the rear of her house and never let her brazier go cold.

She once heard the dog barking at one point, but then heard the man speaking to the dog. She had never heard the dog bark before and it was soothing to know the dog was making sure the man realized that his place was beside the kindling.

The wife and sister made a soft pallet for her in the rear of the house so she would have some place to sleep, while they slept in the wagon. The pallet smelled of fresh straw and soft material, and had a fragrant smell. At night she inhaled deeply of the aroma, never having smelled such perfume.

They still refused any money to procure food for all of them. She offered the family her sleeping quarters, but they refused, preferring to sleep in their cart, but one of the women always slept inside the front of the house, keeping watch over the new mother and her baby.

The daughter always went with her father to the marketplace to sell their wares. She spoke Aramaic very well, but always spoke in their native tongue when the family was together.

She wondered if they thought Yelada would do something to harm the newborn. She had heard that women who were raped would sometimes kill the baby, and there were also slave mothers known to kill their babies to keep them from also becoming a slave. Women who had been raped were also known to kill the baby if they were unable to abort them. To look at the young girl, she did not feel she would do so, but she did not know what type of mindset she had. She did not think this would happen, but then too she also never thought she'd be housing an unwed mother and a baby.

Tahmari and the Pooka daughter discussed her script bags and the daughter explained to her that she was the one who made the bags the family sold. Tahmari gave her a few of her bags that the daughter seemed to like.

Some were beaded and others were embroidered. She did not believe hers were as fine as the Pookas' bags, but was pleased the daughter found them well made.

Early the next day the merchant, his sister and daughter went back to the marketplace to hawk their wares, making sure the mother was comfortable, and returning at dusk. One of the older women who stayed with the new mother would generally be the trader's wife.

On the second full day, Tahmari sat watch over the sleeping mother and baby late that morning and felt sorry for them. She understood loneliness, but to be pregnant, put out of your family home, and not having any friends or a place to go, was something she never considered. She did not know the entire story, only what she had heard from the Pookas.

Reaching over the mother, she picked up the small bundle and kissed the infant's forehead. The baby opened her eyes and made sucking noises, then slowly closed her eyes as she gave a beautiful smile, sighed, and returned to her slumber.

Something stirred in her heart, knowing this may be the only time she would hold a newborn in her arms. Tahmari quietly laid the sleeping baby back into the curve of the mother's arms.

Just when you believe you are in a horrible situation, things could be worse, she thought. She had a lot for which to be thankful – at least she had a home, a bed, food, and clothing. Although they were prostitutes, she also had a few good friends, and even a few good acquaintances, some of whom she could trust.

She found a few of Aunt Halah's clothing in her uncle's old trunk and, having nothing else to do, made alterations to a few so Yelada would have clothes to wear later. The Pookas had burned the clothing the mother had worn and put their own night apparel on her following the birth, which was a bit large.

She noticed the Pooka women called Yelada 'mother' and the infant 'baby'. How odd that the baby was not named. She knew that a husband generally was present for the naming of the baby and, of course, there was none.

She remembered one of her uncle's friend's daughter having the *bris* or *brit milah* along with the naming celebration for a newborn male. Both mother and father, as well as grandparents, cousins and friends had fawned over the baby boy before the mohel-priest anointed the infant's head with oil, performed the circumcision, and proclaimed a name to the baby boy. The ceremony was followed by music and feasting, fellowship and laughter with vessels of wine and platters of food being passed around. Just the thought of the naming ceremony brought a smile to her lips.

Of course, this infant was female, so the circumcision would not take place, but the blessing of the baby and naming ceremony would still have been celebrated. It was sad Yelada was unable to have a naming celebration, but surely a name should be given to the babe, she thought.

As she contemplated her blessings while sitting next to the young mother, she watched as the mother opened her eyes, turned her head toward her and began to speak.

"I want to thank you for taking care of us. I had already decided that I would deliver the baby and die. It was my fault that I became pregnant. I disobeyed my father and decided to go see the marketplace. I am not from here, and wanted to do more than just sit around in my betrothed family's house every day."

"You see, my father brought me here to see a friend of his whose son was to become my husband. I had only met him once when I was younger and even then, I could only think he looked as old as my father. They were in the process of finalizing the betrothal contract, but both father and mother wanted to see me so they could look me over. The two of them looked at me the same way they would purchase livestock, except he did not check my teeth and forelegs."

"At first I didn't mind having to marry him for my father is a very harsh man. He didn't mind beating me or my mother for any reason. I felt this betrothal would serve two purposes—he would have me marry the man to align our families, for his family was very well off, and he would be able to get me away from my home, which would be a blessing in itself."

"However, my so-called betrothed was also a hard man and set in his ways. I don't know if he would be the type to beat his wife or not, but when I asked for a tour of the area, he did not wish to do so. He told me he did not believe in giving tours and a woman's place was in the house."

"After a month of sitting around and doing nothing, I finally left the house and met some people my age, but in the crowds I lost track of them."

"Two men came by and asked if I would like to see a carnival and I said yes, for I had heard of carnivals but never attended one. The one man left me with the other man who grabbed me and knocked the air out of me. I tried to cry for help, but we were in a part of town where no one could hear me. I blacked out and the other man did the same as the first. They thought I was dead because I stopped whimpering and stopped struggling."

"I had heard of animals that pretended to be dead so I did the same. I believe this scared them for they thought I had died. They dragged me into an alley and left me there. I hurt so badly and my body and face were all bruised."

"I crawled my way close to the marketplace where a child found me. The little boy's family washed me, put salve on my bruises. I told them the address of my betrothed so they took me to the house where we were staying. Luckily my mother came to the door and when she saw me, she cried as she cared for me and told me to keep quiet. She kept me away from my father as long as she could."

"We were home for a few months when my mother and I could not keep my condition secret any longer, for it became known I was pregnant. During the trip back here, it was almost my time to deliver and the roads were so bumpy, but my father would not try to make me comfortable."

"My mother sympathized with me, but my father is not a nice man and, truthfully, I hated him. He believed in the rod for the chastisement of me and my mother. I am his only child, but I was not the son he desired."

"When we traveled back to see my betrothed, my father hoped to find out if he would still marry me. When the family saw me and how big I was, they refused. Neither my betrothed nor his parents believed my story. My betrothed shouted to my parents he wanted a virgin, not a used woman." She ended on a sob.

"His father blamed my father for trying to get rid of me with another man's child inside and ended the betrothal agreement. His family still wanted my dowry, which my father had to pay since the fault was on our side."

"My parents were upset and my father beat my mother for not telling him of my condition, then beat me and threw me out of the house. I tried many times to tell him what had happened but he said I had shamed the family, packed up my mother and traveled home. My father said I was never to return to HIS house. My betrothed's family refused to take me in and said my pregnancy was my own fault."

"I didn't know anyone in this area and had no place to go. I was left here by myself. I found an empty house that had blankets and food on the shelves. I stayed there for almost three weeks, but the owner came to check on his house, found me, and threw me out. A very nice widow saw him do it, took pity on me and for a few days took me in. She was already sick, but when she became very ill, her family suggested I leave. They were nice enough to give me a food packet, but that only lasted for a few meals and I still had no roof over my head."

"When you found me in the alley, the pains began and I went into labor. I-I really just didn't know what to dooooo!"

The girl turned her head and commenced crying. Tahmari did not say anything but sympathized with her.

Hiccupping, Yelada looked at the sleeping infant that lay beside her chest and said, "It is not the baby's fault any more than it was mine. It was Yahweh's mercy that brought you near me when I started my pains."

Tahmari lifted her eyebrows, but said nothing.

"Yes," she said with a smile in answer to Tahmari's unspoken question. "Like you, I am Jewish. I saw your artifacts on your shelves so I knew you were Jewish. I know Yahweh will bless you for taking care of us."

She took a deep breath and Tahmari could see she was tiring.

"I'm sorry, really sorry, but I don't want this baby. I didn't even want to nurse it, but the younger woman told me about her sister losing a newborn and I should be happy that mine lived. I know I should be grateful, but what can I do? Now there are two of us who have no home. Although I was with those men for what seemed like hours, I can't even remember what either man looked like and don't even know which of the two might be the father. All I remember is the two of them giggling the entire time."

"I'm sorry I keep crying, but I'm still in the same situation, but instead of just myself, I now have this baby."

"I wanted to thank you so much for taking care of me and the baby. I appreciate you allowing me in your home. Those women and the man have been wonderful to me. They've been talking about plans for me and the baby, and I guess something will happen soon, but only if it is Yahweh's will."

She turned her head and began to sob quietly as the infant rooted its little body toward her breast and began to suck.

Tahmari stood up as Pooka's wife came to relieve her to watch over the two.

~41~

That afternoon, Pooka and his wife came and pulled two stools outside. They had Tahmari sit on one stool as Pooka stood while his wife sat on the other stool. His wife put her hand on Tahmari's thigh and in hesitant Aramaic began to speak. She informed her that mother and baby were sleeping in the main room but they wanted to discuss an important matter with her.

Pooka hesitantly began the conversation, but his wife quickly took over. About that time, the young girl came and stood next to her father as her mother continued. Tahmari believed it was the daughter's job to interpret in the event she did not understand something that would be discussed. She began the conversation.

"My mother said she had explained that my oldest sister is not with us, but with her husband. You see, our Karma lost a baby girl a few months back. The infant died after two days and she is still sad and mourning her baby."

When the mother could see that Tahmari understood the situation, the mother took over the explanation.

"Karma not with us. Her husband want her to stay home for awhile. She need baby to feel better. Yelada willing to give my daughter her baby for she no want it. We ask her to come with us as nurse and be second mother if she wishes. She say she was raped and man she supposed to marry did not want to marry her for she no longer virgin."

"Her father is shamed and put Yelada out. She have no place to go. Father say she had no business going out alone in strange town, which is true. He say family is shamed because of her behavior. Father put bruises on Yelada's back and legs, so he must have beat her."

Tahmari did not know about the bruises and expressed shock on her face. The Pookas continued their story.

"Parents bring her back here and leave her. She not know anybody, so now she want to die."

"We can solve her problem. We talk to her last night. We take her with us, teach her our ways and our language and she will become one of us. She Jew, believe in unseen God, but we not make her change her belief. Our men will make sure she taken care of. Our men good to our women. She will find husband in our village and will be happy. Then she will have baby from new husband and not from unknown man. This will be good for her and for us too—yes?"

Turning toward her husband, who nodded for her to continue, the mother searched Tahmari's face.

"She nice looking, knows how to sew, cook and clean, so any man will want her to be wife. I have handsome son, Batlan. He blacksmith for our village and whole valley. He not married, but need woman, so if she want, she can marry him or another in the village. She make good wife for any man and for Batlan. We'll see."

All three smiled at each other and then at Tahmari. After this conversation, the couple told her the main reason for telling her their story.

"We want you to allow Yelada to go with us."

The entire story boiled down to one thing — they wanted her permission to take the mother and baby with them.

Until their conversation, Tahmari never knew much about the mother. She had never asked. In fact, until the trader told her his family's name, she had never bothered to ask anyone in the family their names and, still, all she knew was Pooka. She tried to apologize to the trader and his wife for her lack of good manners, but the wife waved her apologies away.

"It good you good to woman who have no one."

Tahmari quietly explained that she, too, was raised Jewish and since her uncle's death, she had no one, but she has found friendship. Then she realized, she never gave them her name.

"I'm sorry, I never told you my name. I am Tahmari, niece of my late uncle, Josiah bin Dinkar, and whatever you decide is all right with me."

"Thank you, Tahmari, niece of Josiah bin Dinkar, for being good woman. We take Yelada with us. Is okay, yes?"

Since Tahmari realized they were still asking her permission to let the young mother go with them, she could find no objection. It seems the Pookas had already discussed the matter with Yelada prior to coming to her with their suggestion, so she was more than agreeable. The father had somewhat explained the situation, but now she was more informed.

"Yes. As long as she is willing to go with you, I have no real objection and pray you'll be blessed by having Yelada and the baby in your home. I hope everything will go well with your other daughter as well as with all of you."

It seemed since Yelada was amenable to the Pooka family's suggestion, who was she to not make such a decision? The Pookas seemed gratified by her reply and they all smiled at one another.

On the evening of the third day, the Pooka family cleaned her house from top to bottom, leaving it clean smelling and neat.

Tahmari stressed they should not travel that evening, but stay for one more night, which they did.

The next morning, they packed up the mother and baby and all climbed into the trader's wagon. Yelada had put on one of Aunt Halah's altered robes and looked quite fetching as she held the wrapped baby in her arms. Tahmari realized Yelada's face was now smooth and clear and no longer stressed, for her problems had been solved by the Pooka family.

Within an hour, the wagon rocked a bit as the family settled inside. Hmmm, Tahmari thought, there must be more room inside that wagon than it looks.

It was early morning when the group left her standing in the doorway waving goodbye. When she headed toward her back rooms, she found the sweetest-smelling and expensive incense burning in a small container. Her house had not been so clean or smelled so good since before her uncle passed away.

When she went toward her bed that evening, she found lying on top of her pillows a beautiful silver and gold bracelet, two beautiful silk scarves, and a few gold coins. The coins more than made up for her three and one-half days' lack of business.

The next afternoon, Tahmari once again slid open the door's curtains.

~42~

Months came and went and her routine continued as usual. One afternoon, Tahmari thought she heard her name being called from the front by a female. Since she was in the rear of her house, she called back, "Be there in a moment!"

She had been checking to see if her clothes were dry and began removing them from the rocks, bushes and lines she had set up in the rear. Earlier she had finished washing her clothes in the nearby river. Even if she was in the wrong type of occupation, at least she could wash her tired body and keep her clothes as clean as possible.

She was tired -- very, very tired. Her week had been busy for it had been the Week of the Feast among the Jews. All of the prostitutes had reaped a great benefit this past week for the town had many male travelers visiting. She found the visitors kinder than the men in town. There were traders, Jews from other areas and sojourners to Jerusalem and the surrounding areas to celebrate this special holiday. Now the week was almost over.

As she passed through to the front, she left her dry clothes on her bed. When she came forward, she was met by a smiling Kiri. They hugged in greeting and moved to sit at her small table.

Kiri did not have on any makeup and was dressed in a pretty robe and for the first time Tahmari could see how beautiful she really was. In fact, she looked as if she had lost weight, her hair was smooth and shining, and she no longer looked like a prostitute.

"I almost did not recognize you. Oh, Kiri, you look so beautiful. There is a glow about you. I was going to ask if you were all right, but you look as if you are. You have not visited me in some time and I miss our visits. In fact, you have only been here a few times since Dorit passed away."

Kiri grinned at her friend. "My life has been changing over the past few months, but I wanted you to be the first to know. Turza and I are leaving this area. He has to travel to visit an uncle who is dying. He has been informed by his uncle's messenger that he is the surviving heir, for his uncle never had any children. Turza has asked me to marry him and we will be moving into his uncle's home."

"How wonderful, Kiri! God has favored you with Turza and I know you'll be happy."

Tahmari was so happy for her friend. She knew that Kiri's bruises from her beating had disappeared long ago and she was now in good health.

"I will soon be Jewish, Tahmari, for Turza wants me to convert. I was never very religious and my family worships Molech. There were ceremonial sacrifices offered which made me ill, and even though I was raised in that religion, I could never worship a god that sacrificed babies." Kiri gave a grimace of remembrance.

"But you Jews do not sacrifice children, for which I am glad. I pray I will be able to have children for Turza, for he desires a family, and so do I. Until lately, I never gave thought to having a family of my own."

"Whenever he came to visit me, we'd have wonderful conversations. He would pray for me and I would wait for him to finish praying, but never really thought about Who he was praying to. Now he is showing me how to pray to his unseen God."

"The other day, Turza told me that he has been praying for me ever since he met me. And do you know what he also told me? That he has been praying that I would begin to love him as much as he loves me! I haven't felt love since I left my home at the age of 12."

"If I had stayed, I would probably have been chosen to be what is known as a 'Temple prostitute' and performed sex acts in our god's Temple. My parents were in agreement because to have a daughter chosen as one was considered a family honor although many Temple prostitutes died as a sacrifice or of sexual diseases. Those who ran away would be caught and made slaves or given over to soldiers. At least the Roman vestal virgins did not have sex inside their god's Temples and were well treated. But that was not so in our Temples."

"I survived on the streets and later lived with an older man for a few years, serving as one of his four concubines for he and his wife did not live together and we only went to him when he required us, which was not often for his age prevented constant sex. He was very wealthy and had made provision for his wife to live somewhere else."

"But when he died, his wife returned to put me and the others out. Although he made sure I had money, I quickly ran through most of it within a short time. His wife became a rich widow and I no longer had a home. Eventually, I came here and became one of the town's harlots."

"Turza told me he wanted me to give up this life, and truthfully, I wanted to do so, but what else could I do? After Dorit died, I had visions of dying the same death as Dorit. I began to realize that was not the life I wanted for myself. If I ever have children, I don't want them to know I was once a harlot."

Kiri looked sad for a quick moment and then smiled at her friend. "This is no time to be sad, but to celebrate. I will be married in another town so that when we reach his family, I'll already be his wife!"

"Turza and I will soon be leaving, and I pray your God, and now my God, will also give you a happy life. I'm going to find Luchi so that I can say goodbye to her and the other prostitutes. I really miss Garner, but we all have to make our own decisions."

Kiri turned toward the door and said, "Turza has ordered mules and a wagon and we will be leaving later today."

As they stood from their seats, Kiri gave Tahmari a long hug, kissed her cheeks and whispered in her ear, "I'll always love you and will always remember you, my friend. May our God give us both the blessings we desire."

Kiri quickly headed toward the doorway as Tahmari turned and quietly sobbed. Turning toward her sleeping quarters, she prayed that one day it would be so.

~43~

A few days later, Tahmari passed through the center of town and headed toward her small abode from the well. As she drew water for her vessels, she heard rumors that there was a new Rabbi in town and He was being discussed in every household. His teachings, his ideas, his parables were all that seemed to be on the tips of the people's tongues.

She was told by another prostitute the Rabbi traveled with a group of men, who were his disciples. Were they fellow travelers, protectors of the Rabbi, or men who liked to follow behind someone prestigious? She had seen a few of the men in the marketplace, purchasing food and other necessities. They were pointed out to her by the older women who frequented the well. Was he staying near the Temple as a guest of the priests or in a rented house? Where was He staying? No one mentioned it and she didn't ask in order to avoid conversation with the women.

Truthfully she believed no one really knew.

She continued toward her house. It was not a palace, but because it was hers she felt it was her palace. She looked to the left and saw Samtil, Eliah and Teheran and a few other men conversing together in an alley-way, looking toward her small house.

"I wonder what they're up to?" she thought and continued onward.

She did not trust Samtil, even though he was not one of her customers. Shy Eliah, a minor town official, was not a regular, but the one time he arrived at her door, he paid her what she charged plus a little more and all he wanted was conversation. He did not ask her personal questions or question why she was a prostitute. Yet, there were some men who tried to get more service from her than what they paid.

In the midst of the small group Teheran had his head down, and she knew without a doubt he was plotting something. The only reason she could think that the three might be coming on her side of town was because they were passing through the area. She was not aware that Samtil utilized any of the prostitutes – but who knew?

Dorit and many of the harlots had warned her there were men who were corrupt and would try to cheat them. A few of the prostitutes said even if they were not busy, there were times they would lie when certain customers would approach their houses and say a client was on his way to her house, or that she was having her menses. Although Samtil was not known to frequent the harlots, all said there was something about him they did not trust.

Kiri had admitted he had used her only once and did not try to cheat her, but she always felt somewhat uneasy around him.

"When he came to my house, he asked too many questions about where I came from, what god I worshipped, my family, and so forth. Most of the men come for one thing and one thing only. Certainly not to discuss my life's story."

All the prostitutes said there were times they would entertain men who only wanted to talk or get things off their mind and pay the harlot's price; but such men were few and far between, because most only came for sex, get what they wanted, and left to go home to their wives.

Tahmari had long decided that going into a legitimate trade would enable her to be independent and live on her own without a man. However, after Uncle Josiah passed away, there really was nothing she could do except prostitution. Did she like it? No. But it fed her and made sure she could take care of herself.

She had one customer who asked about her script bag and she showed him a few others. He believed someone gave them to her and she did not refute it. Saying she had others, she went to her back room and brought out a few more. He then offered to purchase them from her and purchased a couple for himself and a friend. He gave her the price she asked, but that was the only sale she had ever made from her craft.

After seeing the Pooka family's bags, she began to make more manly designs. She knew if she practiced she could make some money, but also knew selling a few script bags would not produce a great income.

Tahmari needed the money for she wanted to open a small trade business to sell scarves and jewelry. She knew that in order to do so she needed money to purchase a trader's wagon with one or two animals to pull it. Subsequently she hoped to be able to purchase the scarves and the small stones needed to make earrings and necklaces, as well as stand-alone boards to show her wares. She had saved the bracelet and scarves the Pookas had given her for special occasions, but she had no special occasion. There were no parties or celebrations to which she would be invited and the prostitutes kept to themselves. The only time she had eaten with fellow prostitutes was at Dorit's memorial, prepared by Arbor.

Going into merchant trade cost quite a bit and required a lot of merchandise to sell. When she had enough money, she planned to open her business in another town where no one would remember that she was one of the town's prostitutes. Too many memories were in this small area.

Quiet Eliah never gave her any problems, yet he stayed in the company of Teheran, and Teheran tended to follow Samtil. As city and town officials, they were well-known. However, there was something about Samtil and Teheran that she did not trust. She couldn't quite put her finger on it, just a bad feeling about them when the two were together.

The only others whom she had doubts were the twins, Jaffal and Jakri, whom she dubbed "the laughing boys." She felt everything in life was not funny. They were so immature and it was unusual to see one without the other for they were inseparable as well as insufferable. Generally they followed Samtil, however, today they were not with the town officials.

Again, she wondered, why Teheran was in her neighborhood looking toward her house. She surmised he was probably still angry that she did not allow him in her house. He must have healed from her knife cuts and she was certain he had told Samtil about the episode.

Today was her rest day and she was very glad. Tomorrow was another day and she knew she would once again be busy selling her body.

~44~

Tahmari was scared. More scared than even her first time with a man. There she was—caught in the middle of her sins; her accusers on one side and a strange Man standing alone on the other. He was standing in the center of the raucous crowd outside the Temple courts.

For the past few years she had been prostituting her body with many of the men who were now accusing her of being the obscenities they were now shouting at her. How could they fix their mouths and tongues to call her those words? Such words were not what they called her when they were lying beside her. She knew what she was, but they had never criticized her occupation before.

In reflection, she should have seen the signs. She remembered having seen Teheran, Samtil and others in the alley plotting some strategy to get her into trouble. They were all leaders in the Temple and the town. Those hypocritical Pharisees and teachers of the Law had been whispering and talking among themselves for the past few days, even while coming to her area for what they wanted.

Today, they and some of the men from the village

came to get her while she was with a man. And now, there they were—with stones, ready to hurl at her.

She tried to wrap her now torn robe around her body. She slowly sank to the ground, lowering her body and curling into a fetal position while sobbing hysterically.

It had been their plan to take her naked to the center of town for stoning. The man she had been caught with had slowly realized their intent and quickly picked up her robe. She was unable to grab the small knife she now kept near the bed and knew even if she could reach it, there would be little she could do.

Dorit had expressly told her to make sure her knife would always be where she could grab it to protect herself. Her slow-thinking mind eventually grasped she would have been unable to use it among so many men. Even if she was able to use it, the men would have beaten her senseless in retaliation.

She remembered hearing one of the men whispering to Samtil and a few others, "The Rabbi has left the area of Mount Olive and it looks as if he is heading toward the courtyard to begin teaching the masses."

What did that mean? In all this chaos, why bring a message of that type?

"Right!" she heard someone whisper back, "Let's all hurry to the courtyard."

As they had dragged her from the area near the bed and pulled her toward the doorway, her customer had come forward and, to hide her near nakedness, tried to wrap one of her old robes around her shoulders. The other men pulled him away from her and told him to step aside. She could see it in his face – the man was looking ashamed and apologetic.

She quickly understood he did not know he was to be a part of this charade and was innocent of their deceit – Samtil, Teheran, along with a few town officials had also used him. There were even a few formidable Sadducees and minor priests standing outside her home for they had refused to enter her house.

The customer's name was Aheelim. She vaguely remembered this from her conversation with him before she was pulled from her home. He was new in town and his "newfound" friends brought him to her. It was the middle of the day and she seldom took a customer during that time – they usually visited her in early morning or late at night. She knew that letting them in at that time was nothing but business. She was not so naïve to realize her customers wanted their own sins to take place in the darkness. Most of the men who frequented her house were Jews and married, but that did not stop them from visiting her home.

As she was pulled from the room, she heard the bottom of her robe rip on a piece of loose wood near the door. Being dragged, she stumbled over the small rocks and pebbles that were part of her walkway, for she was barefoot. They dragged her to their destination -- the middle of the courtyard close to the Temple.

It was then she saw Eliah's face looking as if he wanted to cry. Ashamed for his part, his face turned away from her. It was so sad – he could not even look at her. She noticed his hands were hanging at his side, for he carried no stone.

The townspeople knew there were other prostitutes in the area and also knew where each of them lived. A few of the pagan prostitutes even carried on their business in the very area near the Temple. She saw some of the wives of her customers in the crowd. She knew they were aware their husbands frequented the prostitutes' houses of sin, just not which ones.

Strange, the women said nothing, just stared. However, the good Jewish men were yelling obscenities at her. Such language should never be repeated, she thought.

She was the one chosen to be the example for the townspeople, the teachers of the Law, and the Pharisees. This was probably because she was a Jewish prostitute when the majority of the others were not. There were a few Jewish prostitutes who would never reveal which God they worshipped for fear of reprisal from the Jews.

As she cried out for help, no one came forward. There were men at the front of the courtyard's gate waiting with stones, as well as clusters of women trying to see what would happen to her. A few of the women had horror on their faces and others turned away from the scene. She noticed the women with children turned their little ones' faces into their robes as they moved away from the courtyard.

Unbelievable, but her eyes were drawn to a man standing to the side. He was older, taller, his beard longer, but she knew it was Mogdi, whom Uncle Josiah had wanted her to marry. Due to his illness, her uncle was unable to set up a betrothal contract with Mogdi's parents who, she was sure, would have warmly welcomed her into their family. Following the passing of Uncle Josiah, she heard he had become betrothed to a beautiful girl, later married, and now has a small son and baby daughter.

Their eyes locked — hers tearful, his sad. He then looked toward the ground. He did not have a stone in his hand, and once again, she was grateful.

Tahmari felt Mogdi was probably aware of her occupation, but had never visited her house over these past few years. Perhaps he did not have need to visit any prostitute. He was always a devout Jew and followed the laws of Moses. She believed that was the main reason Uncle Josiah would have chosen to set up a betrothal agreement with his family.

Tearfully she spied a few other prostitutes in the crowd, but as she looked at them, they averted their eyes. She saw Luchi, and behind them on the right, she recognized other prostitutes from Dorit's burial. Some of the prostitutes had their veils over their faces and she watched as a few took them off. They knew she was Jewish and felt as a Jew she knew the risks, not just as a Jew, but as a prostitute in general.

At this point, she knew no help was forthcoming. Her fate was before her—she was to be stoned by her accusers.

Which was worse – to slowly die of a horrible disease like Dorit, or be stoned to death?

Her eyes then saw a man pushing forward and realized it was the man, her last client -- the man who was brought to her by Samtil, Teheran and the others. She remembered his name – Aheelim. He had pushed his way through the crowd and now stood in close proximity to the Rabbi. His hands carried no stones.

Funny how the mind works. It just came to her that Aheelim was not looking for any type of intimacy when he arrived. It seemed he just wanted someone to converse with, but Teheran, Samtil and Eliah had given him false information as to where they were taking him.

As a matter of fact, the client was not the one who paid her fee, for she believed the money bag looked a bit heavier than normal. She believed it was Teheran, Samtil or one of the other men who placed the money on the stool near her bed and left.

At first, she and Aheelim sat on the side of the bed and they discussed many things. He seemed to be very nice and was quiet-spoken. He told her some things about the areas he had traveled through before arriving in town.

He was a landowner who, with herdsmen and servants, had arrived after driving sheep and cattle to sell at the market. He said he was blessed by Yahweh because after traveling the long trek with the herds of sheep, he only lost one ewe and a sickly lamb. His shepherds tried their best to save it, but it was to no avail. After sending his help back to his homeland under the leadership of his head servant, he had remained to sell the last of his stock.

It had been his plan to tour the area while taking a well-deserved vacation for a year or so. His men were aware of his whereabouts and would only contact him in the event it was necessary.

Aheelim was not young, but not old either, possibly early 30's. He was of medium height, of a muscular build, soft-spoken and handsome. His beard was well-trimmed, and his yarmulke seemed to have a family design on top. Family designs such as his were generally on the caps of the wealthy, she noted.

From his conversation, Tahmari believed that he was well-read and educated, for he seemed to have a great mind as he discussed the Temple's architecture on his visits there and the town's large marketplace. Aheelim had talked about bringing unblemished animals to the Temple for the priests as part of his and his family's tithes.

She had never heard about people bringing such animals as part of their tithes. She only knew exchanging money for the Temple coins and paying alms to the poor.

She remembered it was she who began to initiate contact by taking off most of her own clothes, trying to coerce him into removing some of his, for he did not seem to be in a hurry as most of her customers. In fact, it was the last and most important day of the Jewish Festival, so she did not believe she would have any customers. She had risen early, gone to the river to wash clothes and was somewhat tired.

Hearing movement in her outer room, she had looked up and suddenly there were men rushing through the curtained area of her bedroom – teachers of the Law, Pharisees and a few townsmen, including those two conniving men. As the men ran into the room, they began grabbing at her near-naked body while Teheran began pulling her by the hair to drag her from the house. Although she struggled, she could not get away, scraping her elbows and knees on the floor as they dragged her.

As she screamed, her customer was so surprised that he did not have a chance to do anything to help. He seemed as stunned as a rabbit under the wheels of a cart. She and her customer didn't get a chance to touch each other before she was pulled from the bed.

Tahmari was so distraught she could only remember bits and pieces of what had taken place and what was now happening before her.

Her mind was now in complete shock.

~45~

The Rabbi had been teaching in the area for a few days and had just come from the Mount to the courtyard when the men dragged her forward. He and his disciples looked at the crowd of men, watching with interest the townspeople on the periphery.

Pushing her forward, Tahmari almost fell at the Rabbi's feet. She slowly righted herself and put her head down, avoiding the people's stares.

The Man in front of her was not one of the Sanhedrin or wore the clothing of a high priest. His robe was richly made, but not flamboyant and he had well-made sandals on his feet. Although though the arguing body of men showed him respect, she could feel their dark currents of disdain.

"Rabbi," Samtil had shouted as he pointed an accusing finger in her direction. His hatred of her was causing him to tremble in anger.

"Here is our town prostitute, a Jewish prostitute!"

Beside him stood Teheran, who nodded his head in agreement. They were accusing her as if she was the ONLY prostitute in town.

It seemed this Rabbi had just reached the courtyard when she was brought before Him. She had heard there was a new Rabbi in town. With her downcast eyes, she saw only a circle of feet and sandals when she realized that they had called him 'Rabbi.' He did not look like any of the other teachers of the Law. He was not stern of face or scowling like the Sadducees, and did not seem pompous at all, like the Pharisees.

Samtil hand came back and threw a small black rock to the ground, which bounced toward her. When this happened, many of the men were aghast. The black rock is only used in the courts, proclaiming the accused as being guilty. If the person was found not guilty, a white rock would be thrown.

But there was no court. There was no trial. There was no defense.

"Rabbi," a voice called out, "this woman was caught in the very act of adultery."

How dare him! Without looking up, she knew by the sound of his voice the identity of this accuser.

Teheran! Why she had seen him only a few nights before. Not just him, but she could identify many of her clients' voices in the crowd. Some she had even had recently in her house.

"The Law of Moses says we should stone such a woman. Now, Rabbi, what do you have to say about this?"

Every Jew knew that answer! What a stupid question

to put before a Rabbi. Even pagans knew the answer to that question. Yet, the group of men continued to question Him about religious laws, as if they wanted to trap Him.

Why would these men ask such a question? She was sure all Jews knew what the Law of Moses said about prostitutes. If he was a Rabbi, would He not know the answer?

Tahmari could hear the men shouting more obscenities, and haggling among themselves and a few even began picking up stones with their hands. Such rabble! It seemed some of the men had even brought large stones with them as they came toward the courtyard.

The men seemed to be waiting as Teheran and Samtil maligned her before the Rabbi.

Tahmari did not see them, but could hear the voices of Jakri and Jaffal giggling in the background. Everything seemed to be funny to those two, even to the stoning of a prostitute.

She kept her head bent forward causing her hair to hang over her eyes as she prayed that her stoning death would be swift.

Jesus acted as though He was not interested in their words and gave no answer to their questions. Tahmari knew her accusers were waiting for some type of response from Him. She did not believe He answered any of their foolish questions.

What exactly were the questions? Questions about the laws of Moses?

In her confused and shocked state, why couldn't she understand what was really going on? How was this Man a part of their plan? Was her fear so great that she had missed something? If she didn't prostitute her body, however was she to live? No one gave her money to purchase food so she had to fend for herself.

~46~

Tahmari was once a beautiful young girl. She had large dark brown eyes with long lashes, long dark silky hair, but her hair was now dirty, tangled and matted. The skin underneath was smooth, but one could not tell what she really looked like because her eye makeup of kohl and olive cream had coursed down her cheeks.

Having lived with her uncle since she was a child, Josiah ben Dinkar had raised her to be a gentle young woman. After his death, life had hardened her to be what she had now become.

When Uncle Josiah became ill and finally died, she was left alone before she could be betrothed to her childhood friend – the young man her uncle had picked for her— Mogdi. They had played together as children. Mogdi was protective of her and when they played games, he would sometimes let her win – until she became just as adept. He would pull on her long braid and laugh until she slapped away his hand. He was a great friend and Uncle Josiah knew he was the type of young man who would take care of his niece.

Leaving her with nothing but the small house she lived

in and no dowry to speak of, Mogdi was later betrothed to another and soon married. She was alone and on her own, for she had no husband or brother or any male to care for her. The only thing left to do was to beg or sell herself.

Tahmari remembered begging alms outside the Temple and was told by the guards and doorkeepers to leave the area. It didn't matter that no one wanted to give her alms, for people could see she was not blind, crippled or infirmed. She couldn't even sell her wares. She had made jewelry and clothing, but people would only purchase the foreign goods sold in the marketplace. She had nothing else but her body.

The life of a prostitute was not an easy one. Some of her customers would not give her the entire service amount. There had once been a man who left her home without paying. Garner was the one who taught her it was best to require her fees up front. She couldn't even go to the magistrate to try to get her money for she had no man to vouch for her. And who would listen to a woman—let alone one of the town's prostitutes?

Friends – no! Her uncle was well-respected before he died, but his niece meant nothing to his friends. The doctors had taken their money, and still Uncle Josiah did not get well. It was bad enough the women of the town would do nothing to help her.

Now, because of her occupation, the girls with whom she grew up would have nothing more to do with her. If they took any notice of her at all, it was to roll their eyes or turn their heads to avoid looking at her. Some would even turn and walk in another direction so as not speak with her.

She did not have enough money to move to another area, and even if she did, she was still a woman without the protection of a man. That was when she decided to go into merchant trade, but that took a lot of money, which she did not possess.

Too bad she was unable to join the security of the Pooka family like Yelada.

~47~

The Rabbi quietly looked at her and then at the accusing group of men, while giving a slight smile. Tahmari did not see his smile for she had put her head down. She did not see the compassion in the Rabbi's eyes as her accusers awaited His response. He touched the top of her head and she raised herself to a standing position, still keeping her head down.

What a touch! It was a soft touch, as of a loving father to his daughter; or a loving uncle to his niece.

Instead of answering right away, the strange Man stooped down and began to write in the ground's soft dirt with His finger. She could not see if what He wrote were words or symbols -- for tears blurred her vision.

Very quietly and calmly the Rabbi stood up and the men quieted as He turned to look at them. He let his eyes roam slowly over the gathered men. It was almost as if he was searching into the hearts of each one. Some of the men shifted from one foot to the other. He did not answer their questions or ask one of His own, but made a statement in a low, but firm and resonant voice.

"If any one of you is without sin, let him be the first to throw his stone at her."

That was all He said.

Right away the atmosphere became highly charged and no one seemed to breathe.

Tahmari cowered while still trying to wrap her tattered robe around her body. She wrapped her arms around herself to await the first barrage of stones. She had heard that men always aimed for the head when throwing stones, then to the chest or back.

Her life was based on the Rabbi's one quiet sentence. It was more a statement than a question.

Again, the Rabbi stooped down and once again began moving his finger as if He was writing something special in the dirt.

She turned her back to the crowd and continued to weep. Through her sobs, she could not hear any response to his statement.

~48~

Suddenly, she realized the atmosphere had changed and the scuffling sound she was hearing was the sound of feet moving away. She barely heard the thuds as some of the stones were dropped to the ground.

The men left, one by one—the older men first, and then the younger. They began leaving the area so that within a few short minutes only she and the Rabbi were left alone. He moved His hands together, wiping away the dirt, then slowly stood up and touched her shoulder.

She looked questioningly into His eyes as He gave a slight smile, keeping his hand on her shoulder while looking into her face.

"Woman," He asked, "where are your accusers? Is there no man here to condemn you?"

She could scarcely breathe. She hesitantly turned and looked around. Where were the men who had dragged her to the courtyard? There were stones all around on the ground where before there were men with them in their hands. Turning back toward the Rabbi, she looked up in the face of her savior. His eyes! His eyes! Love and compassion smiled through His eyes.

They were alone in the courtyard—no accusers, no crowd—just she and the Rabbi.

"There is no one to accuse me, sir," she quietly answered.

"Then neither do I," He calmly gave her another slow smile that lit his eyes as he instructed her, "Go my daughter, and sin no more."

The Rabbi then turned and headed toward the other side of town with his disciples following. She noticed others followed behind him. There was a man in the crowd of followers she recognized, and at first could not figure out why he was familiar.

Why, he was the same man who had approached her on crutches outside the Temple when she was begging alms. One of his legs had been shorter than the other and he had to lean on his crutch to talk to her. He had pointed out that she was not infirmed and should go to the women's section to beg.

And there he was standing straight and tall as if nothing was physically wrong. She remembered one leg was shorter than the other and now both legs had been made whole.

At first she hesitated, her eyes showing their gratitude, but afraid some of the men might return to come after her, Tahmari wrapped her robe around her body and ran.

Quickly she left the courtyard and headed to the near outskirts. Running past her home, she quickly passed the tall boulders outside the area and found refuge in one of the caves on a low hill.

Huddling in the darkness of a small cave, she cried while praising Yahweh for saving her from her fate.

~49~

At early evening prior to sunset, she ventured quietly around the outer edge of the courtyard and headed for her small home. The little dog was lying beside the outer wall, but moved away as she approached. Tahmari put her forefinger to her lips and gave a quiet "shush" to him.

She pushed her way into the house, where a table was turned over and her bed was sideways near the door. There were drag marks in the dirt where the men had pulled her out.

The smell of sex lingered inside and she wrinkled her nose. How odd that she had never noticed that odor before. The last time she could remember her house smelling clean and fresh was following the departure of the Pooka family.

Gathering clean apparel, she began putting on warmer clothing and a pair of her old sandals. She then placed more clothes as well as a couple of blankets, into a large bag. Putting what little food she had in a smaller bag, she crept back to her cave while dragging her items with her. Traveling slowly with her burden, it seemed her few items became heavier and heavier before she reached the cave.

After depositing her belongings and resting for a short while, she quickly returned to her home to grab the few mementoes that reminded her of Uncle Josiah, hair pins and jewelry, and as many small items she could carry in another bag. Tahmari made sure to retrieve Uncle Josiah's scrolls for they were precious to him as well as to her. They were in a woven bag and she carried them carefully with her.

She was surprised to see the money the men gave her was still on the stool near the bed, so she quickly seized the pouch. She also had some money she had saved in a small pot, including the coins and items given to her from the Pooka family. She found the beautiful scarves and sandals she had not so long ago purchased and put them in a small packet along with a few candles and flint. Seeing some of her jewelry and beads, she placed those inside the pocket of her sleeve.

She began swiping the footprints she made in the dirt with a leafy branch and hurried back to her cave. She did not want to leave any tracks someone might see and be able to follow.

Along with her other earnings, she wrapped her saved funds in sheepskin and hid it under a large rock inside the cave. It became apparent this might be her home for some time until she could figure out what to do or where to go.

It was now dusk and the sun was beginning to set so she quickly picked up two small water pots and once again left the area to draw water from the town's well. She looked around to make sure no one saw her and hurriedly took the filled vessels back to her cave, careful not to spill much of the precious drops.

Tahmari began digging in one of the bags and grabbed a small pot of salve which Arbor had given her and sat on the floor of the cave. She lit a broken candle to see better in the darkness, and after checking out her bruises and skin scrapes, she began treating her cuts and broken skin. Her elbows and knees were scraped raw from being dragged, but was grateful the salve was soothing to her skin.

Laying her thin blankets in the small alcove of the dirt floor, she fixed a small living area for herself. Going further into the cave, she dug in the dirt dog-style a hole to set up a small brazier for heating. She doubted she would need a fire for cooking.

Once again, she scampered outside, gathering wood and small branches to be set against an inside wall to make a small fire before darkness completely encompassed the area. She found flint and decided she would not start a fire right away, but perhaps later. She did not want any smoke to give away her hiding place.

Praise Yahweh, the night was not very cold! When the stars began to shine, she was able to see a little and began setting up firewood for a small fire. The fire and her blankets kept her comfortable.

She knew she should eat something, having brought a little food, mostly stale bread and cheese. It didn't matter whether she ate or not she realized, for she had no appetite. She checked the entire inside of her cave, making sure there was not another exit where animals could come inside. She placed a thick branch from the gathered firewood and a few large stones against the cave's opening for protection. If an animal came, would she know what to do?

Her fear was captured in all of her senses. Her ears caught the sounds of the wind. The taste in her throat was bile. Her nose wrinkled as she smelled decay from old leaves and possibly dead rodents.

The darkness was lifted only by the small fire she had made in her makeshift brazier, yet her palms were almost as sweaty as when the circle of men had surrounded her. Twice in one day, she closed her eyes and thought to herself, was this the culmination of her life?

Throwing back her head, she screamed aloud, "Oh, Yahweh, please protect me! I know I'm a sinner, but please don't leave me alone!"

Hearing a low whine, she knew the little dog had followed her. Ahhh, she thought, the comfort of another lonely soul.

She had no place to turn, no one to help her and it seemed even Yahweh had removed His presence from her.

Sobbing, she curled into a fetal position and stared toward the cave's opening.

The sun had completely set, her candle had gone out, and it was now very dark. She tried to get some sleep for she was extremely tired. The stress of the day had exhausted all of her energy, yet she found it hard to sleep. All she could think about was the happenings of the day, the strange Man they called 'Rabbi', and the fact that she was still alive.

As she thought back over the events of the day, she covered herself with a blanket and cried herself into fitful slumber.

~50~

Something awakened her.

Disoriented, she looked toward the cave's opening and saw there was a full moon, providing a small stream of light inside the darkness of the cave while the stars glittered around it. Tahmari then heard a scuffling noise outside her cave and knew that was what had awakened her. The noise was too loud to be the little dog and she began silently praying.

Quietly she threw aside her covering, arose from her makeshift bed and grabbed a large rock from the pile she had placed nearby. She picked up the rock in one hand, holding the other hand against the cave's wall where the large branch had been placed, and slowly moved forward. As she tiptoed toward the opening with one hand drawn back, ready to throw the rock, a man's shadow slowly appeared from the reflection of the moon. The man's shadow seemed to grow larger as he approached.

"Miss, miss," the words were whispered, "are you there?"

She was not sure who it could be. She had a horrified thought. Oh, no – lepers! This cave may have belonged to a leper. Lepers lived outside the town and frequented the caves. She had not thought of that aspect.

In the moonlight, the shadow lengthened sideways as the man came nearer to the cave's opening. She recognized his voice as the man who had been the customer.

"What-what do you want?" she whispered in return.

"I came to apologize. I am so very sorry," his voice was contrite. "I had no idea what those men were doing or even that they were planning to stone you."

"Go away," she cried. "I no longer plan to service anyone. I am to sin no more. I am no longer doing that. Go away! Please go away!" She was very nervous and her words stumbled over each one.

A bit louder, she said through the opening, "You should know that I have a weapon!"

She bent down and picked up another stone that fit into the palm of her other hand, but the man's shadow did not leave. In fact, it seemed to come closer to the cave's opening.

Silence.

"How did you find me?" she finally whispered.

"After you ran from the courtyard, I became worried and realized you would not go back to your home, but I went there any way. I saw that some of your personal items were no longer there, so I knew then you would not stay there. Then I saw you late this evening and followed you from the well after you filled your water pots. I just wanted to make sure you were all right. I feel guilty about the entire incident and waited until nightfall to come. Just so you know, I made sure no one followed me."

"Umm, my name is Aheelim," he said, as if that would bring his identity to mind.

Of course she remembered him.

"Please go away, sir. I-I need to be alone right now." She slipped back into the darkness of the cave.

When she heard a bit of scrambling, she thought Aheelim would try to enter the cave and raised both hands, preparing to throw her rocks, but she realized he was backing away from the entry.

"Thank you for checking, but please do not let anyone know I am here," she called out.

"I-I-ah, I brought you some food," he whispered, "and will leave it near the opening."

The shadow slowly retreated and then he was gone.

After a time, when she heard no noise, Tahmari timidly crept toward the cave's opening and saw a small sack. Upon pulling it inside, she opened it and found cooked fish, fruit, goat cheese and fresh barley bread. She bit into the fish and quickly chewed pieces of the cheese and bread. She had not realized how hungry she was and shoved the food into her mouth quickly. She grabbed the gourd near her water pot and scooped up some water, gulping hurriedly.

Eventually slowing her eating, she savored every

morsel. Knowing the mongrel was near the cave, she placed bits of food for him to eat and some water in a small bowl, deciding she would save the fruit and extra bread and cheese for breakfast in the morning.

She was not sure how long she could stay in the cave. True, she had become somewhat comfortable in a short while, but there were wild animals in the area, plus the homeless and lepers might come by.

When she finally lay down on the floor of the cave and covered herself with her thin blankets, she was so exhausted she fell into a deep sleep. At one point she dreamed Samtil, Teheran and the Pharisees were outside the cave shouting and pointing their fingers at her. Even in her sleep, the fear was there, but then she saw the Rabbi, whom she later learned was called Jesus, a Nazarene teacher from the area of Galilee. He and Aheelim, as well as the small dog were chasing the men away.

The dream ended but she felt somewhat comforted and, although fitful, did not dream the rest of the night.

~51~

Following the scene in the courtyard, Aheelim had sat on one of the chaises in his rented house. He mentally went over the details of the day: He remembered bumping into the same woman a few days back, when he could see she was being followed, but she did not accept his help. Then today, he was taken to the place where she practiced her trade.

He knew it was a plot for her to be stoned by the corrupt men of the town, along with the Pharisees and the city's officials. What type of town was this?

Aheelim did not care for the men who grabbed her, the official named Samtil, the thinner one who grabbed her hair to drag her from the house, or the two silly men he had met earlier. He was not surprised to see the crafty stock merchant who wanted to make a profit off his sheep. That man had a small stone in his hand, possibly because he did not know the prostitute, but decided to join her accusers. Was it possible he was also a part of the subterfuge?

Aheelim had now met the Rabbi, a Man he had wanted to see and meet in person. He was amazed at how Jesus had judiciously handled a volatile situation. He had heard of Jesus the Teacher, Jesus the Rabbi, as well as Jesus the

Healer, and was now able to see Him as an advocate. He could see He was full of wisdom by the way He studied the crowd and quietly showed great judgment.

Getting up from his chair, he stood in the doorway and saw movement of a woman's shadowy profile stealthily heading toward the well. As his eyes adjusted to the dusk, he saw it was the prostitute.

On a whim, he decided to follow her without her knowledge as she left the well. He had earlier gone to the courtyard to see if he could find anything of what Jesus had written on the ground. It seems the Rabbi must have wiped away whatever it was, and there were now numerous footprints across the same spot made by the townspeople as they had later walked over it.

He saw the woman heading toward the outskirts of town and followed her, noting her going inside one of the smaller caves. Noting the location, he then returned to his rented house. It bothered him that she was alone. Hmmm, he thought, she undoubtedly has no family or a protector. No relative came forward to offer for her.

He had a hard time falling asleep as he thought about the day's events, the young woman, and the cruelty of the townspeople.

Tahmari. That was her name. Tahmari. It was a name almost like sigh. And such a nice looking woman at that.

◆

Over a few days' time, Tahmari knew Aheelim was the one who had been making the visits to her cave, for he had begun leaving small items outside the cave's opening each night – food sometimes, a small pillow, and even a scarf for her head. She noticed there was even a small bowl of meat she believed was for the little dog.

Since he was the only one who knew where she stayed, she knew the gifts came from him, but she was still wary. After seven or eight days, she had stopped having the horrible nightmares and had begun to sleep less fitful. She ventured out only to replenish her water supply or relieve herself, going to the small pool in the evenings to bathe, all the while making sure she was alone, except for the dog which seemed to stand guard over her clothing.

She made a point to remain unobserved, seldom meeting any of the townspeople. The little dog was the only one who noticed her as she came and went, and he would disappear when she entered the cave, later returning to lie outside the opening.

Tahmari smiled for the dog was her only friend and security. She always made sure to feed the little animal from the food Aheelim placed near her cave. He only growled once and that was when a small rodent came too close to the opening, making the animal skitter away.

◆

It rained on and off for a day or so, and during those times, Tahmari remained close to her cave. The area around her cave was a wasteland, barren. Barren like her heart. Very few bushes, hardly any grass or plants and everything was brown and gray. Already depressed, she would sometimes think of her uncle and cry for some time.

Unbeknownst to her, Aheelim had heard her sobs as he dropped by to deliver more sustenance. He would quietly back away from the cave when he saw the little dog lying near the opening, but the dog never barked or growled at him as he deposited food. Somehow he knew the dog did not want him near her when she cried.

He supposed the dog was trying to protect her and give her the opportunity to grieve. A few times he heard movement of the night animals which roamed the area, realizing should any wild animals happen to come near, the small dog would not be of any protection.

Aheelim found he could not sleep, knowing she was out there. He knew it was not his presence that dreadful day that caused her to be used, for he knew he had also been used. For two nights, he tossed and turned, thinking about a lonely woman living in a dark cave in the wilderness.

Aheelim had nodded half awake and half asleep, trying to see how he could help her. Fearing for her safety, Aheelim arose from his bed, sat as the table and began to form a plan.

~52~

About ten days after the courtyard episode, Aheelim arrived early one evening and stood at the cave's entry carrying one large sack and two smaller sacks. He spoke quietly to her as he told her to pack her items inside. He had another smaller bag to which she added her sheepskin packet of money, jewelry, and other personal items.

"The darkness and cold are coming upon us quickly now, so it is best you leave your cave. There are many wild animals which sleep in holes and caves around this time of year and you should not be hiding here. Besides the beggars and lepers might move in with you and surely you don't want that to happen," Aheelim pointed out.

"I'll come back later and remove your other items from the cave so no one will know you occupied it. Things a leper can use I'll leave there, like your water pots and blankets."

"I have found a place for you to live for a time. We will leave here when darkness falls. Leave your leftover food for a leper in the event one decides to use this cave. If not, the animals will forage and be grateful that it was left for them."

"Here, leave those clothes and put on this robe for it will keep you much warmer than what you have. It gets cooler at night."

When Tahmari touched the robe, it was soft and smelled heavenly.

"Thank you." Not knowing what else to say, she began to comply with his instructions. In a short time, Tahmari was ready.

She put on the robe and tied the scarf he had given her around her head in the event someone would see her. The scarf was as fine as the ones she received from the Pooka family. She also noticed Aheelim's clothing was of fine material and believed him to be a wealthy man, but he was very down to earth and didn't put on any airs like the pompous officials or well-to-do men in town.

When Aheelim deemed it dark enough, she followed him unobserved to the other side of town, both of them carrying the bulging bags to a small comfortable house.

There was a small fire in the brazier, making the house very comfortable against the now cool evening. The house contained beautiful tapestry, and various furniture items. In another room, there was a table, a couple of chaises along with two chairs behind a makeshift desk, a large upraised mat for lounging and an area for clothing. It also contained a curtained area to the left which she thought might be for his other personal items.

Two candles were burning low on a table giving muted

light, an area for relief with a chamber pot, and a smaller room in the rear of the house for guests, she supposed.

"Welcome to my home," he said. "Of course it is rented while I transact my business, but it is home to me," he smiled as he waved his arm around.

"Oh, no," she backed away from him. "You don't understand. I cannot stay here. Please, please, I don't do that anymore."

He looked at her strangely, and then understood.

"Don't worry. I do understand. I didn't bring you here for any shady purpose and you don't have to worry, for I will not touch you in an intimate manner. The men who brought me to you do not know where I am staying. It worried me that you were alone in the wilds and I felt guilty because of my part in your capture. I wanted to make it up to you."

Tahmari looked around and he believed she was trying to find the entrance to run away. She began blinking back the tears that had formed in her fearful eyes.

"No, sir, you really don't understand what I'm saying. You'll get into trouble. The town's officials, Pharisees and scribes are evil men and will take out their vengeance on you. You see, some of them would come to my house at night as customers and they are the same men who planned to stone me. They would do the same to you if they could."

She was at the point of crying for she did not want him

to get the wrong idea about her and she certainly did not want to get the man into trouble.

Aheelim moved quickly to stand in the doorway, blocking her escape, to make sure she did not run outside.

"No," he said. "Please listen to me. Your services were not the problem with those men. They used you and me for the express purpose of trying to get the Rabbi into an argument about the Law. We were just ploys in their game. It was not my intent to have relations with you. I was looking for a certain tradesman when I met them at the town's gates. As we were walking along, they took me to your house. When I arrived, I realized what type of house it was."

"By looking at some of the bowls and candles, I also noticed that you are Jewish. I have found in my travels that there are very few Jewish prostitutes. That seems to be why you were chosen out of all the other prostitutes."

"They could have picked any prostitute, but it was not in their plan to use a pagan prostitute, for the pagans neither worship Yahweh nor follow our Jewish laws."

"You are Jewish and they put you on trial because you have chosen to be a prostitute. Remember, the scribes and officials never mentioned the name of the man with whom you were caught, for I never gave them my name or where I was staying."

"The Rabbi used remarkable discernment and saw through their plan. Even a non-practicing Jew knows what the Law says about prostitutes and yet, there they were asking foolish questions of a Rabbi, a learned man of Yahweh's laws nonetheless."

"They lied when they told the Rabbi you were 'caught in the act' of adultery. Even though you were scantily clad, I was not undressed. And too, we never had any relations."

"You see, their purpose was one of deceit. Those town officials, the scribes and Pharisees should all be well versed in the Laws of Moses and should have known the answers to their own questions without testing the Rabbi. I could tell He knew what they were up to. He was very astute, which is why He said that those without sin should cast the first stone. I believe He knew some of them had been customers of this area's prostitutes, even before they came to Him."

Aheelim slowly said, "Don't ask me how He knew, but I could swear He knew."

"I had heard of Jesus of Nazareth before he came to this area and have been listening to those who have attended His teachings. One thing I do know and that is the Rabbi is a good Man, and I believe He was sent from Yahweh."

Tahmari looked questioningly at him. "I know very little about this Jesus of Nazareth, only through rumor and gossip by the women in the marketplace. But I do know He had compassion on me, a prostitute and sinner."

She was quiet for awhile, and then said, "I wonder what He wrote in the dirt. He never said and it was strange that no one asked."

Aheelim began to fill her in on what had taken place during the scene in the courtyard and afterward, as well as how the men looked at each other when Jesus questioned their sins. Each one of her accusers was shame-faced.

"They were cut to the heart by their consciences for they knew their own sins. Even I began to question my own sins."

Aheelim started setting out the food he had purchased for the two of them, and as they ate, he explained how he had been going to the Temple to listen to Jesus teach. He could see that Jesus was not like the other teachers of the Law and spoke to them in a way that all could understand.

"There was a man who had one leg shorter than the other and the man's crutch slipped from under his arm as he tried to see what was going on. Jesus caught him before he fell and held him by the elbow. Next thing we knew, the man's legs were normal. I don't know if anyone even realized that Jesus had healed his legs. The man did realized it and began jumping up and down."

Tahmari became excited. "I noticed that man too. When I tried to beg alms, he came to me on his crutch to let me know I should not have been there. Jesus must have healed him!"

"I sat under his teaching in another town but not very close. Here in Jerusalem and the areas surrounding Galilee, he has been very visible at various synagogues and the Temple. He tells us about our Father, Yahweh, and how we are loved by Him. It was almost as if He was talking about Yahweh on an intimate level, as if He was his Son."

"The priests and teachers of the Law only tell us of the punishments if we don't do certain things. He explained Yahweh's grace and mercy and lets us know how we are blessed. Oh, just so many things. I could sit at His feet and listen all night long."

Aheelim clasped his hands. "It is said he heals all who come to Him. I'm quite sure He healed the crippled man."

"I understand He will be teaching on the hills outside the town for some time. We might be able to attend and see for ourselves."

Aheelim nodded his head and she did the same. However, Tahmari felt a bit of trepidation at his remark. If she met up with the Rabbi, would He remember her and her sin? She did not wish to be seen in public just yet, but kept her thoughts to herself.

When they finished eating, Tahmari began clearing the dishes as Aheelim talked about Jesus' teachings and how he had met some of the people who have been healed by Him. He related stories he'd heard about Him healing demon-possessed men and about the dozen or so men who traveled with Him. Since Aheelim traveled a lot, he had heard quite a bit about Jesus and His miracles and believed that He was the long-awaited Messiah that had been spoken of by the prophets.

When she would interrupt him to ask a question concerning the Rabbi's messages, Aheelim would become animated while answering and would gesture excitedly with his hands.

At nightfall, he showed her where he had set up a place for her to sleep in a small curtained room where she would also be out of sight if someone were to visit his home. There was also a night robe and although large, it was comfortable.

When she settled into the bed, she gave a low moan of pleasure. The bed was the opposite of the cave's floor, so soft and comfortable. For the first time since her uncle passed away, Tahmari felt secure and safe and did not toss and turn before falling into a restful sleep.

Aheelim quietly pushed the curtain aside and watched her sleep for a few moments, then re-closed it, laid some items out for her use in the morning, then went toward his own sleeping area.

~53~

Tahmari awakened late the next morning and was surprised to see a bowl of warm water, a small cloth, lye soap and oils. On a small stool was draped a very nice robe, another scarf and a bone comb for her hair. At first she was hesitant to use the robe and scarf, but since her other clothes were either left in the cave or unfit to wear, she washed and put the new clothes on. She presumed Aheelim had disposed of the ones she had worn in the cave.

When she came from behind the curtain that was used to separate the rooms, Aheelim was surprised to see how young and lovely she now looked without the garish makeup and smelly clothing. The stress that had been on her face was not there. No one would now recognize her for the same harlot in the courtyard.

"Just want you to know that robe was used by my youngest sister. For some reason it was included in my case. Generally I would find some small memento from her. When she was little, and even until today, she has always had a habit of including something in my bags to remind me that she loves me and I should think of her whenever I'm away on a long trip. Instead of a piece of jewelry or one of her sandals, I would find a scarf or an earring. I guess she must have thrown in the robe. It's way too small for me, but came in handy for your use. I see it fits you very well. We'll purchase a few extra pieces of clothing for you later."

Tahmari smiled her thanks realizing her few pieces of clothing were the clothes of a prostitute. They were not where she left them the night before and surmised Aheelim may have thrown them away, or even burned them. She did not want to ask what he did with them, but appreciated what he had been doing for her.

After a quick morning meal, Aheelim began small talk with her as she cleared away their debris. They discussed mundane topics, the weather and events and activities of the town people. She could tell he was avoiding discussing what she did for a living and her courtyard experience.

Over the course of a few days, their conversation became less stressed and she opened up about her life with her uncle. Aheelim was a great listener, never questioning her, but allowing her to tell him more of her life.

~54~

She and Aheelim fared well together and there were times she would feel his eyes on her. He never attempted to touch her and for that she was grateful. She would often find herself following him with her eyes, but did not want to take their relationship any further.

Aheelim continued purchasing food for the two of them and when she tried to give him some of her money he refused.

"I have more than enough money for what we need," he would tell her with a smile.

To repay him for his kindness and without being asked, she cooked, cleaned and washed for him. He had not asked anything of her, but complimented her each day. The arrangement was a good one and she was grateful. It brought back memories of when she performed housekeeping duties for her uncle.

One day Aheelim reported he was able to sell most of his sheep and cattle. He said he had help from a friend named Goshen, who worked at the livery in town.

Less than a month later when he announced that his business transactions were nearing completion, Tahmari began to feel uneasy. She knew this secure relationship could not last forever, but decided not to dwell on the fact that one day he would leave.

She and Aheelim began attending Jesus' sermons when he taught in the Temple and on the hillsides. Once He taught in an area near her cave and she noticed the little dog coming through the opening and heading toward the now gathering multitude.

Tahmari mentioned to Aheelim that the dog was always around. She had never had a pet, but there was something endearing about the little dog that was comforting. She believed it was because whenever something upsetting happened, he was always nearby.

Tahmari thought back to several occasions where she had previously noticed the dog: She believed he was the same puppy she had observed when her uncle passed away. At the well when she met Kiri. At Dorit's burial. When she was followed by Teheran and how she had laughed as he raced after Eliah and Teheran following her attack. He even waited with her when she ran from the courtyard after her near-stoning.

"Perhaps that dog is your guardian angel sent to watch over you and you have yet to realize it." Aheelim laughed at his own supposition, but Tahmari pondered this.

She and Aheelim would talk well into the night afterwards for both believed Jesus to be the Messiah. It was rumored that the chief priests and Pharisees wanted to have Jesus assassinated, but Jesus seemed to always be a step ahead of their plans.

Supposedly, the chief priests had sent Temple guards to find Jesus, but He would be in a certain place one minute, and somewhere else the next. It was as if Yahweh Himself was spiriting the Rabbi away from whichever area they looked.

Tahmari and Aheelim spied some of the Temple guards and doorkeepers in the crowds on the hillsides listening as Jesus taught. Her eyes met the eyes of the Temple guard who had to remove her from the begging area and he smiled and winked at her. She was not surprised that the guard recognized her because she remembered he said he knew her in her youth. She gave a great smile as he looked at the man sitting beside her. He gave a nod and turned back to listen to what the Rabbi was saying.

The scribes, Pharisees and priests believed the guards refused to arrest Jesus as they had been instructed. There would be no assassination by them for the Law stated "you shall not commit murder."

Truthfully, the Temple guards felt Jesus had not committed a crime and many were becoming believers. If the Roman guards did not disperse the crowd, as they were wont to do, why should they?

Tahmari continued to go to the well late in the day when the last of the women would be leaving. No one seemed to remember the prostitute at the edge of town and she realized that no one recognized her, for her appearance was now changed. When she was a prostitute, some remembered her as the woman with a lot of makeup and the jewels on her scarves. She was eating well, had put on a few pounds and was no longer the skinny woman with a lot of makeup. Her skin was youthful and soft once more and with the clothes she now wore, she was left alone.

For a while, a few of the older women would try to look her in the face, but she continued to keep her face down or turned to the side. She found it was best to not start a conversation with anyone. She was now unrecognizable by the townspeople, even running into some of her long-ago friends, but made no attempt to speak to any of them.

One morning when she was purchasing food items at the marketplace, she ran into Shallum's wife, Marka, who attempted conversation with her, which was unusual, for she was not known to speak with anyone.

Perhaps she had no friends to converse with, Tahmari

thought, but at the present time she felt it would be best to be cordial and not carry on a conversation that would eventually become questions.

Tahmari just nodded her head and moved away. Strange, Marka never spoke with her before, did not attend the Shiva or funeral for Josiah, yet here she was trying to look into her face and start a conversation.

She knew Marka did not recognize her for they had never had anything to do with each other, either in her youth or as an adult. Because Uncle Josiah had given her warning, she kept away from Marka and no longer visited the marketplace early in the day.

One afternoon, as she and Aheelim were sitting at the table talking, they heard shouting, screaming, and the footsteps of people running toward the opposite end of town. They also smelled something burning and as they looked out the door, could see black clouds of smoke rising in the far area of town. Aheelim left her and ran behind the flow of people.

Although she had a dark feeling, Tahmari did not move. She remained in the house and was still sitting at the table when Aheelim returned.

Crestfallen, he came back some time later and sadly informed her that her house had been burned to the ground. Since no fire had been left burning in her house for the couple of months she had been gone, they agreed that either the town officials, the Pharisees or the townspeople had probably set the fire, eliminating all traces of the prostitute who used to live there.

Tahmari remained stoic, showing no remorse or anger in her face. She was, however, silent, not saying anything, but very happy she had gone back to her house to retrieve her money and the few personal items that reminded her of her Uncle.

Unbeknownst to Aheelim, Tahmari was not sad because the house was gone, but he noticed only that she portrayed no emotion at all. He thought she might have been in shock. He did not want to tell her that parts of the house could have been saved, but no one tried to put out the fire. He had observed this as the townspeople stood around watching it burn – no one moving to remove items from the house.

He was also aware that no looting had taken place. Some people were so desperate, they have been known to run into a burning building to see if there were pieces of furniture, jewelry, money, or something they could use in their own places. There were even those, including lepers, who will look for food on shelves, but that did not occur. He was told by a few people standing around that it looked as if the fire started from inside the small house, which meant someone had to have gone inside to set it afire.

Aheelim recognized the only one concerned about the burning house seemed to be the little mongrel. He sat to the left of the house and sat on his haunches moaning as the little dog watched the place burn.

After that, Tahmari's house was not mentioned in any of their conversations—it was as if the house never existed.

~56~

Goshen stood at the door with a smile on his face. He was surprised to see a woman kneeling near the brazier, putting a few sticks of wood into the small fire. He could see she was not doing any cooking, but was feeding the small fire to keep the house comfortable. Seeing his shadow, the young woman glanced up in surprise.

"Good day sir, may I help you?" she asked.

"I was looking for a man named Aheelim, who is my friend. Did he leave this area?"

Goshen looked a bit uneasy. This was not his first visit to Aheelim's house and he did not know Aheelim had a woman living there, for he had never seen or mentioned a wife, and did not seem to be the type to take in a mistress. He did not believe her to be a sister, although Aheelim had mentioned to him he had many sisters. Still, he found this woman to be very pretty. He had been to the house a few other times and Aheelim was always alone.

Suddenly, Aheelim was standing behind him and clapped him on the shoulder.

"Ah, hah, so your shoulder has healed. It is always good to see you, Goshen. You are looking very well and

I see you have added a few more pounds to your thin frame."

After inviting him inside, Aheelim introduced him to Tahmari as his very good friend. Tahmari nodded her head as she shyly gave him a smile and quietly left the room. Goshen thought it best to not ask any questions. He knew about men of wealth who sometimes kept a mistress or concubine besides having a wife, or those who liked to have beautiful female servants surrounding them. Growing up, he even knew of one well-to-do citizen who also enjoyed sexual favors by young slaves, male and female. He was grateful that he was never owned by such a man.

"What can I do for you? I see you're still working with Abner and whenever I would check on my animals, he would tell me how pleased he always finds your work."

Aheelim did not explain the woman's presence and, therefore, Goshen felt it was best to not ask personal questions.

Blushing, he nodded his head when Aheelim suggested he have a seat near the table he used as a desk.

"I wanted to ask your opinion on two matters, sir. It concerns my work and a woman for whom I have developed feelings." Again, his face flushed even redder.

"Could this be a certain Tirshah I have met the few times I've seen her at the livery? I understand she is Abner's niece and is quite lovely. You introduced me to her the first time you began working there."

"Yes, that is her. She is lovely, isn't she? She has lived with Abner since her parents went on a trip and never came back. It is believed they died going into a dangerous area for no one has heard from them. She said her parents were not the type of people to just leave their children. Abner is her mother's twin brother and he knows nothing about betrothals. She and her brother, Pashur, have been raised by him since they were young. I need to know how to go about asking her to marry me."

"She feels she has passed the age of betrothal and Abner has not given a thought of her wanting to marry. I know I'll be able to take care of her because Abner just found out I have been trained in tannery and smithy."

"Someone brought a mule to him loaded with animal skins and asked about a tannery. When he was told there was none nearby, I volunteered to help the man. It's a laborious and foul-smelling job, but I finished it within a month's time. In fact, I did such a good job that Abner suggested we set up a tannery in the rear of his property and I would be able to set my own fees, but I'll have to think that part over because it is very hard work and the smell does not leave your body even with soap and oils. Yet I do so love working in the livery and stables."

"I told him I had also worked as a smithy before and the next thing I knew, Abner set up a small area for smith work. He has been singing my praises to his customers. With the new smithy area, I already have a few customers. I have made a great deal of money just doing a bit of smith work, and I've been teaching Pashur to be an apprenticed smithy. I believe he enjoys that more than livery work. I told him that eventually he will become accustomed to the smells and the heat, but we might later develop a partnership."

"I would rather do blacksmith work more so than tanning but as I told Pashur, it doesn't hurt to know more than one skill."

"I know he'll allow me to marry his niece if nothing else but for my skills, but I don't know how to go about asking for her in the correct manner. I have been studying with Abner and am now a Jew, you know. Did I tell you I have converted and am learning Hebrew? Tirshah explained to me about the Hebrew area of Goshen. My name is a great name and I thank you for giving it to me. I pick up languages and dialects and can interpret for his customers. Abner is also pleased that I asked so many questions about Jewish history in the teaching classes."

Goshen put his head down and quietly confessed, "I hope you don't mind, but I did sort of hint to him that you had started teaching me your history and he was happy about that."

Aheelim smiled, but did not comment. He knew Abner would never allow his niece to marry a pagan, so it was good Goshen was admitting he was not pagan or Gentile.

"Tirshah has also taught me Jewish history, the Laws of Moses and the Commandments. I have been attending services at the Temple and observing the holy days along with her family."

Goshen then took a deep breath and then asked, "Aheelim, can you or will you help me?"

Aheelim stood and hugged Goshen. "You are a knowledgeable man and I am sure you'll be great at whatever you decide to do. You'll find our history is a good thing to know, but I believe you are gathering faith in our God, and for that I am pleased."

"Of course tanning hides is really smelly and you might want to decide performing blacksmith work so when you come home, your wife will still want to hug you or you'll never have babies."

Aheelim had to laugh at his own joke and Goshen joined in.

"As far as asking for Tirshah, I will speak for you if you wish. But first, you must find out if she wishes you to be her husband. Does she have other men courting her? She is very pretty and from what I see, I believe she does have feelings for you. She knows you're an ex-slave, so you should have no problem explaining your background. And don't forget to add that you were once my slave, although for a very short time, in the event she asks."

"Also, Goshen," he chuckled, "you do not have to tell her about a knife being put at your throat for stealing food!" Both men laughed about that episode.

"First I will build a small house to attach to Abner's land because she would be hesitant to move away from her uncle. This way we will have some place to live when we marry, and perhaps obtain extra land to add more rooms in the event we have children."

Aheelim was amazed at his plans. "Well it seems to me you have worked everything out on your own, but I don't believe you'll have a problem asking for Tirshah as your wife. Come and walk with me and we'll discuss these matters."

~57~

She and Aheelim were heading toward an area of town where it was reputed the Rabbi would be speaking. The couple followed the crowd of people traveling toward the hillside. On the way, a large merchant's cart rolled past them, then suddenly came to a stop halfway down the road. Aheelim looked back and saw a short man, a tall young man, and four women jump from the cart to run toward them.

"May I help you? Are you looking for a certain area?" He was confused because all six people came toward them with a smile on each face.

"Pretty lady, pretty lady," the shorter man was yelling. "Tahmari, halooo, Tahmari," he screamed.

Then all of them began yelling Tahmari's name. Aheelim was confused. Who are these people and how do they know Tahmari's name?

Upon hearing her name, Tahmari had hesitantly turned, girded her robe and began running toward the six people.

"Oh my, oh my," she screamed, "it's the Pooka family! Hello, hello!" As she ran, she continued screaming her greetings to them. Aheelim realized she must know these people, who undoubtedly, were merchant traders.

The group met together in the middle of the road and began hugging and kissing Tahmari's cheeks and hands. Aheelim was quite surprised at the familiarity with which they greeted each other.

Tahmari held her hand out to him to draw him closer to the group.

"Yelada, you look so well. You've gained a bit of weight and your skin is so soft and smooth."

The younger woman gave a great big smile, grabbed the hand of the taller man and pulled him forward to introduce him to her.

"Tahmari, I am now a Pooka and am married to a most wonderful man! The Pookas are leaders in their town and I am now a part of a family. I am treated as a princess because my father-in-law has announced to everyone that I am his new daughter. They love me, Tahmari, they truly love me. Now I know what a real family feels like!"

All of the Pooka women had tears in their eyes as they hugged Tahmari, and the smaller man kissed both of her cheeks. The sister took both of Tahmari's hands and held them against her face, while Yelada wiped happiness tears from her cheeks.

"This is my new husband, Batlan. The Pookas are my new parents as well as my in-laws and they are wonderful."

She was breathing heavily from running and her words scrambled over each other.

"They are allowing me to sell my script bags that I have created. I am even allowed to keep a percentage of the money I make from their sales, for Batlan and I are saving up to build a larger house. He built a small house behind his parents' property and, until he married me, had no need to expand. One of his rooms has been made into my crafts room and now we are beginning to need more space."

"He does not care about me having a baby from the rape, Tahmari, and the baby now belongs to his sister, Karma. Now that Karma has my baby, she is doing well. Batlan and I are second parents to her and we hope to soon have children of our own."

"That's wonderful, Yelada! I am so happy for you both. And how is the baby doing?" Tahmari asked.

"Little Tahmari is doing very well and is now walking and talking. She is becoming very adept at learning two languages."

She gave a happy smile when she saw Tahmari's raised eyebrows.

"When my mother-in-law said I had to name her; Karma and I could not think of a good name, until we thought of the kindness you showed me at her birth – allowing me into your home and taking care of me. Karma asked your name and I told her and she liked it. Then we decided to name her after you to thank you for all you've done for me."

"If you hadn't been walking by at the right time, heard me in labor and found the Pooka family, I don't know where I would be. We've been looking for you these past few weeks. We went to your house, but it is nothing but barren land. We heard it caught fire and burned to the ground and we are so very, very sorry. It was a nice house."

"We almost passed you by, but my father-in-law recognized you first, then the rest of us. You look wonderful!"

The family beamed at her and Tahmari returned their smiles. She almost forgot Aheelim who now stood beside her.

"I am so sorry; please forgive my manners. Let me introduce you to my friend, Aheelim. Aheelim, please meet the most wonderful family!"

Aheelim had been standing silently to one side, marveling at the change in Tahmari. He hardly recognized this outgoing young woman as she greeted her friends. Her cheeks were flushed and her eyes glowed with pleasure, making her seem much younger than before. He smiled at the family, giving a slight bow as they chattered to him about how Tahmari saved the young girl's life, mentioning a baby that had been named after her, and how the girl, Yelada, now has a husband.

He hoped that sooner or later, Tahmari might explain to him the entire story.

Yelada opened Tahmari's fingers and placed a beautiful script bag into her hand. It had the most colorful design she had ever seen and the needle work was raised, similar to brocade and beads.

"What a beautiful bag," Tahmari marveled. "Wait! There's money inside!"

The younger girl laughed. "Yes, the bags you made and gave to my sister-in-law sold quickly and I wanted you to know that your work is good. The coins inside are your profit. Keep up the good work, Tahmari! And by the way, we copied your designs too!"

Laughing and smiling as they took their leave, the Pooka family began climbing back into their merchandise cart, as one by one, the two men and three women hugged and kissed Tahmari.

The last to do so was the fourth and younger girl, Yelada, who whispered something in Tahmari's ear. Whatever words she whispered made Tahmari smile, but some of the light went out of her eyes.

The two women once again began crying as Yelada climbed back into the cart. Smiling and waving with the smaller man driving, the cart swayed as the family traveled toward the other side of town.

~58~

"You seem to be having a great day," Aheelim surmised.

"I have always wondered what became of Yelada," she answered. "She deserves all the blessings she is now experiencing. Yahweh has been so good to her, showing her the favor she did not receive from her own family, especially since before there was nothing but horror and sorrow. The Pookas are a wonderful family and I'm so happy she now has a loving husband."

Aheelim started to ask about the baby, for undoubtedly the child was not Batlan's, but he did not want to pry into Tahmari's personal life, and felt if Tahmari wanted to tell him the entire story, he could wait.

As they walked, Tahmari gave a slight giggle which then turned into a chuckle and finally she began to laugh.

"What's so funny?" Aheelim could not understand the humor.

"Before she got into the wagon, Yelada whispered some thing in my ear and made a funny statement. She said, 'You know, I laughed at the name Pooka, and now I am one of them. Tahmari, I am now a Pooka!' I also had to laugh because when the father introduced the family's name, I too thought their name was quite funny. Yelada also whispered ...," she hesitated, started to say something else, but stopped. "Oh, never mind."

She gave a slight shake of her head and continued walking, but he noticed that a smile remained on her lips.

~59~

Tahmari continued to go to the well to retrieve water at about the time the last of the older women would leave. Again, no one seemed to remember the "prostitute on the other side of town" and was pleased to realize no one recognized her.

During the past few months her appearance had taken a change for the better.

She saw Marka a few times, but she chose to not start a conversation with her. Marka did not try to push her presence on her and eventually left her alone, possibly thinking she was new in town.

There were times she would run into some of the town's prostitutes, but none bothered to speak with her, possibly because of her changed appearance. Prostitutes seldom looked any of the townspeople in the face, so she was aware they probably did not recognize her. Or, she no longer wore her prostitute's scarves and veils. Even some of her clients did not bother looking at her in the face and, without her beaded veils and garish makeup, she was unrecognizable. As far as the townspeople were concerned, she was just another young woman.

One day, while at the well, she overheard a small group of older women discussing the capture and deaths of two men who had tried to rape a young girl behind the marketplace.

"I heard this girl was around the age of 12 or 13 and was from a well-to-do family. I guess they were visitors in the area for they were traveling through town. There was another young girl walking the area who was almost raped a few weeks ago, but she was able to get away. About a year and a half ago, a young girl was raped and I guess her family took her home because very little was said about it. No one knows the girl who was attacked, but the rumor is that her parents sent her to another town to recuperate."

"One thing that is always mentioned by the girls is that the men just giggled constantly. It was reported the two were twins. Something had to be done to these men and I'm glad the Romans took care of it."

"The Romans? What about the Romans? What did they have to do with it?" Tahmari could see the audience was aghast as they prodded the older woman for more news, to which she happily complied.

When she was a child she would walk with her aunt to get water from the town well and listen to the day's gossip. She remembered Aunt Halah telling her that the woman with the gossip was "queen" for a time and her audience was her court. The woman with the best gossip was known to hold her audience spellbound. They had laughed heartily at that.

The small group of women was giddy with this news and prodded the older woman on, for they wanted to know every single bit of this news.

The "queen" knew she had her court enthralled for she ignored their questions as she proceeded to continue her story.

"It took place two days ago. This last child had been on a shopping trip with her brother and a large male slave as chaperones and the sun was ready to set. It seems the child's chaperone had left her with her younger brother for a few minutes beside one of the merchant's stands to wait for him while he went to relieve himself. Within the few minutes he was gone, the two men grabbed her from beside the girl's brother, who began yelling."

"When the slave returned, he saw the brother had been knocked down by one of the men and the two were trying to drag the screaming girl toward an empty building. One had his hand over her mouth trying to silence her screams and the other was trying to lift her feet to make it easier for them to carry her away."

The queen paused for effect and began using her gesturing hands to help with her description.

"Oh, my," interrupted one of the other women and a few of them had their hands to their cheeks in horror.

"I can't believe such things have been happening in our town."

"I always make sure one or the other of my sons travel with my daughters since these rapes have been occurring. With all the prostitutes in this area, you'd think evil men could get what they wanted from one of them, not from young virgins!"

"Oh, yes," the queen continued her story, "and supposedly the slave returned to the cart just in time, and when he saw what was happening, he ran behind them shouting and yelling for help. He caught up with them and began fighting them. A few other men in the area came to see what was happening and when they were told the two men were trying to rape the girl, they joined in beating them."

By this time, Tahmari was listening along with a few more newcomers as the queen continued her tale. She believed the woman who was talking began increasing her volume to make herself heard knowing the crowd had grown and there were others listening to the side.

"They knocked down the two men and began pummeling and kicking them." She stopped talking and began moving her fists and feet as if to explain the punches.

"I heard the brother placed his sister aside into the protective arms of two women and even though he was young, joined in the beatings. It is said the chaperone was a well-built Phoenician slave and was used to fighting his enemies in his own country, so I'm quite sure he did a fine job on those men. When the gathered crowd found out what was happening, more men came to help with the beatings and all began hitting and kicking the abductors."

"Later, it was said that one man told the Roman soldiers he joined in beating the two because it would keep his own daughter from being a victim and he was making sure it would not happen to her."

Catching her breath, she started to continue her tale, but was interrupted by a woman in the back of the crowd.

"The two men didn't get away, I hope."

"Oh, no. Even if they tried, they were grossly out-numbered. It was about that time that a Roman troupe of soldiers patrolling in the area heard the noise and screams and ran to break up the mob. One of the two rapists tried to fight back by drawing a knife on one of the soldiers, but the soldier wrestled the knife from him and during the scuffle he was stabbed and killed. The other man was beaten very badly by the mob and it was reported that he died within a few minutes or so."

"What happened to their bodies?" one woman asked.

"I've been told the soldiers dumped their bodies some-where on the outskirts of town." The queen took a deep breath and released it while saying, "Let the wild animals and the bugs finish them off, I say—which is what they surely deserved!"

Nodding their heads in agreement, all of the women wholeheartedly did a general discussion of what they had just heard. Within a few minutes, the crowd of women began dispersing to their own homes with filled water vessels and something to discuss with their families over dinner.

Tahmari listened to the entire story and was very surprised when she heard the rapists were the twins—none other than Jaffal and Jakri, known to be upstanding citizens.

Although brutal, perhaps it was best they died because who knew what would have happened to them otherwise. The Romans have never shown mercy to the lawless, Jewish or pagan. Rapists especially were known to be punished in a gruesome manner, sometimes stoned, sometimes run through with spears, castrated, crucified or burned alive. Sometimes all four. And since they fought with Roman soldiers, it was a wonder they weren't decapitated for the soldiers' weapons are very sharp and dangerous.

Oh, my Lord! Tahmari thought. Could the twins be the ones who raped Yelada? Could one of them be the father of her baby? It came to mind a statement she had heard that some men enjoyed using the same woman for sex. She thought they were talking about two men having sex with the same prostitute at the same time. Yelada also mentioned they seemed to find her struggles humorous and everyone knew the two men were constant gigglers.

Had Jaffal and Jakri been abducting young girls throughout the past few years? Why young virgins? As one woman had stated, there were more than enough prostitutes in the town with experience of how to satisfy a man. She knew there were some men who only wanted a young prostitute. She knew that when she first began her harlotry, some men came to her because of her 'youth and fresh face', as one man had admitted.

When she returned to the house, she and Aheelim discussed this latest news. Aheelim said he had also heard of another young girl who was almost kidnapped, but she could get away from her two abductors by kicking in the groin the one who tried to hold her feet. When he doubled over, he let go of her and she was able to run.

Again, that young girl could not identify her abductors, only that there were two of them who kept their head down and both giggled throughout her struggles.

~60~

The couple continued traveling toward the hill area where it was rumored Jesus would be speaking. As they crossed over a small indentation in the ground, Tahmari almost tripped, but Aheelim was there to catch her.

"Easy there, young lady. Am I going too fast for you?"

His concern was encouraging. He held to her elbow and waited while she fixed her sandal strap which had come loose.

"No, I'm fine. I saw that little slope, but I was in it before I could correct my stride. Thank you for keeping me upright."

She smiled at him, noticing he had not released her elbow. Her heart sang for the warmth of his hand was reassuring.

"How about walking closer to me in the event you decide to trip again," he quipped.

Slowly he released her elbow and they began walking side by side. Soon they began to see more people and which gathered into a crowd, and they knew they were going in the right direction.

Jesus was situated on a slight incline and his voice was able to travel so that all could hear him. He discussed the "Father" as if he had personal knowledge of Yahweh. If He was the Messiah, Tahmari could see that He had such knowledge. He did not ask for money or fame, but instead of worshipping Him, he asked that the listeners worship His Father, Yahweh.

Tahmari sat on a small boulder with her hands in her lap as she listened intently. She chanced to look at Aheelim with her peripheral vision and saw that his eyes were looking straight ahead and he was smiling and nodding his head as he agreed with what was being said.

Suddenly he turned and caught her surreptitious look and gave her a prolific smile.

As their eyes locked, he patted her hand and said, "I believe in my heart that this man is the Son of God. Otherwise, no man could speak like that. And did you take note of the man who was on crutches and how he is no longer on them. The man next to me said Jesus asked the man to come forward and healed him. Now the man is able to sit on the grass with no help from anyone."

"Before we arrived, I was just told that He healed everyone who came to Him who were sick or afflicted. Some people were upset that after their healings, those people would not leave the front area. But, you know, if I was just healed from an infirmary, I would want to be as close to the Rabbi as possible, too!"

Tahmari agreed with him and both turned once again to listen to the Man on the hillside.

As they began the return trip to Aheelim's home, she began talking about her early childhood, Uncle Josiah, and how she came to be a prostitute. He was surprised when she admitted that she had to give her tithes to one of the middle-aged men who frequented her house.

She admitted he was a nice older man, who did not always wish to lay with her but wanted companionship, because he had no real friends he could confide in.

"He once admitted to me that he was a widower and had no family in town. He did not feel safe discussing his personal business with the men he knew. Also he would receive messages and notes from businessmen and sometimes family members, and asked me to read them to him—for his reading skills were not the best. Once he found out I could read, he would bring his messages to me."

"We had an arrangement that when he wanted to just sit and talk, I would not charge him, but he had to keep my secret. He was a good conversationalist and we would discuss many things. There were a few times when he and I would read the scrolls together. In return, he would take my tithes to the Temple."

"Although he didn't have to do so, he would still put money on my stool."

At Aheelim's quizzical look, she added, "Yes, although I'm a prostitute, I still try to be a good Jew by fasting, saying my prayers, paying my tithes and not doing any work on the Sabbath and holy days. The giving of my tithes and not working on the Sabbath are some things I strictly adhere to. I may be in the wrong profession, but I know how good Yahweh has been to me. I've been blessed in other ways, really too numerous to count."

"Prostitutes are considered sinners, which I am – was – and my money would not have been accepted in the Temple."

He looked at her strangely as some of what she was saying began to sink in.

"Wait! What? You can read? Who taught you to read? Your uncle?"

"You seem surprised. Yes. One of my clients found out when my script bag fell off my table, which contained my writing materials and he realized I was educated. My uncle taught me to figure, read the scrolls and even how to throw a knife, among other things. He did not have any children of his own so I was taught boy stuff and things a male should know, even to reading the scrolls." Tahmari gave a satisfied sigh.

"In fact, this client came to me for some time but had never seen my face. He would finger my veils because I put a few jewels, designs or stones around the edges. It is the Roman prostitutes who tend to put names on their veils and bands, but being Jewish, I refused to do so. I still wear my veils and am known more for the beads and jewels on them, than for any other identification."

"After we became more familiar, he began coming to me to talk or have me read his letters. With his eyesight beginning to wane, it was getting harder and harder for him to see the words. When I finally began to trust him, I took my veils off and we became good friends. He has never divulged my secrets nor have I divulged his. My uncle once told me a good friend would never tell your secrets, so I should never give away my friend's secrets."

"Uncle Josiah was a wonderful man. We had a housekeeper named Meka, and as I grew older, she taught me the female things I should know. Every once in a while I would go with her to help deliver babies, but I only performed mundane chores. I never actually held the babies after their birth except I do remember holding one as the midwives wrapped the child in swaddling, but for only a few minutes."

"Uncle Josiah would stammer and stutter when I asked about the changes taking place in my body or anything having to do with female things, so Meka and I would go for walks and she would explain such things or answer any questions. Meka was a great friend, but she moved away and I only recently learned she passed away."

Thinking about Meka made her a little sad and put her head down to fight the tears, but brightened a bit when she happened to look up.

Aheelim whispered, almost to himself, "You're educated!"

"Don't look so surprised." She had to laugh because of the look on his face.

"There are other females who are educated, but we don't usually spread that around. Women are supposed to only be domestics – knowing how to keep house, clean, cook, raise babies, and take care of the man of the house. Those types of things. And I can do all those things and others because my uncle and Meka taught me. Oh," she added, "except perhaps raising babies since I've never had any. In fact, Yelada's infant is the only one I was able to hold in my arms for more than a few minutes."

Aheelim began to laugh. At first it was a low rumble, then a chuckle, and then a guffaw. Soon he was bent at the waist and laughing loudly. Every day he was learning something new about the woman. He finally hiccupped as he tried to stop laughing and began wiping his eyes.

"I am so very sorry, Tahmari. I'm going back to the part about you being educated. I just didn't think of you as one who reads – and a reader of the scrolls yet! You are surely something!"

They laughed together, and then Aheelim stopped and looked at her.

"Tahmari, do you like children?"

"Of course, although I hadn't given much thought to them. I loved Yelada's baby, and felt sorry for the infant because at first the girl refused to allow the infant to nurse her, nor did she want to give the babe a name. How odd to now find out she named the baby after me."

She gave him one of her radiant smiles.

"I've been blessed that I have not gotten pregnant myself, and I keep track of my days. I was advised that getting pregnant was bad for business, because then I would wonder which man was the father."

Slowly Tahmari told Aheelim the story of Yelada and her rape. She explained her relationship with the Pookas, and why she was so happy to see them again.

"I could almost understand Yelada's predicament, for she didn't know which of the two rapists might be the father and she just wanted to forget the entire episode. The baby kept it foremost in her mind, for the baby was a reminder. Now that she has given Karma her baby, and she has Batlan for a husband, things are looking up for her. When Yelada becomes pregnant this time, she will know who the father is."

They had slowed for a short time and suddenly he grabbed her hand and put it inside his arm and they commenced to walk companionably together.

At a safe distance, the little dog followed behind them.

~61~

A month or so after the fire, a young man came to the door to find Aheelim and bringing him a message. He remembered the young man as one of the men who helped unpack his load when he arrived in town. He smiled as he gave the young man a few coins, sat down, quickly scanned it, and then looked at her.

"It's from my man of business. It is imperative that I leave here and return home. It will take a week or so to get there, so I'll have to leave early tomorrow morning," he said quietly.

Tahmari's heart stopped beating for a few seconds, but she nodded and said nothing, then turned and silently went through the curtained area he used as his private quarters and began packing his clothes and items in the leather bags he had brought with him.

He followed a couple of steps behind her as he wrote a few notes on the back of the message. On his way out, he looked at her and smiled.

"Don't worry. Hopefully I'll be back within a few hours to help with the packing" he announced, and hearing no response, left the room.

As he left, Aheelim noticed the small dog lying outside the door of his house. The dog had gained some weight since he and Tahmari had been feeding him and looked healthy with his now shiny coat. The dog stood and came close to him waving his tail back and forth. His entire body exhibited joy when Aheelim bent to pet him.

Tahmari had told him the dog did not belong to her, but he believed she was pleased to have his comforting presence since she had no friends or family.

◆

Behind the curtain Tahmari wanted to cry, realizing tears were fruitless for she had no say-so in his doings. He had the right to come and go as he pleased. By now they had developed a familiar routine which she knew was bound to end one day, although she had hoped it would go on much longer. Tears ran down her cheeks and she felt her heart was heavy. Even her legs felt wooden as she dragged her feet while moving around behind the curtain.

It was her own fault she had begun to have feelings for him. Sitting down on the small chair by the door, Tahmari put her head in her hands.

Again, Dorit's words ran through her mind.

"Try your best not to develop feelings for your customers. For that is what they are, ladies. It doesn't matter if you call them clients or patrons, for they are still your customers."

Realizing she had a lot to be thankful for, she thought back to her first meeting with Aheelim. He was the kindest man she had ever met outside of Uncle Josiah. Aheelim was a few years older than herself, but he had wisdom far beyond his years. A man possessed of warm humor, he was also studious and well-read. He considered his words before he made a statement, something she found to be a noble act.

Aheelim was concerned for her well-being in many ways, starting with when she was being followed. He even asked if he could walk her home for her safety.

His kindness was extended when she was pulled from her bedroom with next to nothing on. He tried to cover her nakedness, handing her one of her older robes before the men could drag her to the courtyard. She had not realized how important that was to her until just now.

She remembered spying him in the crowd as he parted a group of men in order to place himself closer to the Rabbi, and he did not have a stone in his hand.

He was concerned enough to discreetly follow her at night from the well to find her hiding place and he even made a point of bringing her food so she would have something to eat while in the cave. In fact, he even gave her extras for the little dog.

Aheelim was concerned and compassionate enough to want to keep her safe by not wanting her to stay in the cave because of what might befall her if she remained, mentioning the animals and lepers who frequented the hilly area. Then his act of kindness by bringing her to his lodgings was more than helpful and to this date he has asked nothing from her.

When he said he would not touch her, he had lived up to his promise by not taking advantage of her presence in his home and she did not feel compelled to go against what the Rabbi told her. He gave, but expected nothing from her in return.

Tahmari believed Aheelim mourned the burning of her home more than she. She heard through the town's rumor-mill that her cousin, Shallum and his wife, had the debris cleared away, and had taken possession of the property. This was only right, so they were her kin.

Since the courtyard fiasco, things that used to mean a lot to her no longer did so. She had learned to appreciate the smaller things she had been taking for granted, never considering things could, and would, change.

She knew she had only Yahweh to thank for these many blessings.

What she would do now was another problem. Where would she go and how was she to exist?

Slowly she stood, wiped her eyes and continued to do the packing for a most wonderful man.

~62~

When Aheelim returned from completing his business transactions, they ate their meal in silence. She, because she had nothing to say, and he, because his mind was on the business at hand.

As she cleared the table, he said he would now have to leave in a few days because he still had business to complete and it looked as if it would be two more days. Tahmari set aside extra clothes since there was now a delay on his leaving.

Tahmari praised the Lord and savored those extra days in her heart.

Before he had shepherds and other servants with him to keep his herds of sheep and cattle in line and he had traveled behind a few days later. This time his travel time would be much shorter.

Tahmari put some of his clothes on a stool, along with his traveling sandals to wear in the morning.

She arose early the next day and following a quick breakfast, Tahmari began cleaning their living quarters so that the house could again be rented by the landlord.

Aheelim went to his quarters, reached under his pallet and pulled out a small box, three pouches which would carry his small personal items, and his script bag. Taking them with him, he finished his business transactions before heading toward the livery to collect his mules to bring them back to the house to complete the packing.

They went to the marketplace, purchased roasted fish, fruit, beans, and fresh vegetables. He said he didn't need to pack a lot of food as some might spoil and there were nice inns along the way.

Once again it was getting dark, which slowed his departure time. He mumbled more to himself than to her, "Tomorrow is another day. Early morning is the best time to travel."

Tahmari awoke early the next morning and began packing the last of Aheelim's items before preparing a small meal for breakfast. Aheelim said he had to do one more thing, would return to eat and would then be ready for traveling.

She completed the packing and filled a bag of animal skin with meat, cheese, unleavened bread, as well as a skin of water and another of unfermented wine.

Tahmari really did not know where "home" was since they had never talked about it, but in her heart, she knew that once he went home, he would not return. In the meanwhile, she could not think of where she would go or what she would do.

She had known Aheelim's business would eventually be completed, but hoped it would not be until much later.

Later was now here. If it had not been for the messenger bringing the note, he would have remained in town much longer.

In her mind, she contemplated going to Garner's old house, but she was not sure she would be welcome since she did not know the new owner. It would be hard to find a place to stay since she no longer sold her body.

Dorit was dead, Kiri and Garner were gone. Arbor traveled with his new master, and she had never been inside Luchi's place. And after everything that has happened, would Luchi allow her to stay in her house? She wondered if the new owner of Dorit's house had moved in yet – would she be able to live there for a few days. Probably not.

She would also have to purchase new veils and makeup and try to find another house if she went back to her old way of living.

But the Rabbi had told her to sin no more.

That was easier said than done. However would she be able to survive?

In no time, Aheelim was back. Tahmari showed him the packed items and food for his trip.

"It was my intent to start out early, but when I went to finish receiving the last of my funds from the sale of my animals and to pay the final rent to the owner of this house, that business took much longer than I thought. It is now first light. I went to the livery and have retrieved the mules and my horse, which are in back, but now I'll have to travel at dawn. Early tomorrow I'll begin packing the mules so that business will be over with."

Suddenly Aheelim drew a chair near the table and sat down, but Tahmari stood nearby. He waved his hand toward another chair inviting her to sit, but she continued to stand in front of him.

He began explaining to her the contents of the note he had received. She wondered why he wanted to discuss its contents with her, for his business was his affair and, after all, he would be leaving soon.

As Tahmari stared at him, he again waved her toward the chair and she finally sat. He held the missive in his hands, while tapping the table with his other hand and continued to speak.

~63~

"When you're a landowner and have a lot of servants, it seems they tend to argue a lot among themselves and with the servants of other landowners. Why those men argue even more than my sisters. And believe me, my dear, I love them all dearly, but my sisters are all different. How my father puts up with them is beyond me." He began to chuckle as he spoke.

Aheelim made himself more comfortable in his chair and set the missive in the middle of the table. He tapped it with his fingers and began to explain the problem.

"It seems my shepherds have been arguing with my neighbors' shepherds about the three new wells we had dug before I left. When I asked if the other landowners wanted to dig a few wells on each of their properties so we could all have water and share any water we find later, they declined. Now, it seems they and their animals are coming over on my property to use my water." "My men do not want to share, and I understand their position. Now I have to go home to settle the argument. It was my intent to share the water, but my men feel the others did not want to help them when they began digging for the water, but now they are using too much."

"My servants are correct and I agree with them. As soon as I arrive home, I will discuss with my neighbors the fact that previously they declined the offer of my men to help their men dig their wells."

Tahmari turned that information over in her mind.

"You should not let them continue to use your wells, for they need to be independent of your property. I would suggest you charge them for the use of your water until their wells have been dug. The landowners should have their servants dig for their own water, so perhaps charging them would make them begin digging their wells right away to avoid expending any money."

She felt she was being too forward and stopped, but Aheelim nodded, waiting for more comments, so she continued.

"If they don't, then I would suggest you halt their infringement, especially since you say you would offer your men to help them dig their own wells, but your men should not do the digging themselves. It is only fair that their servants start digging and should they need extra help, then you could make your men available to help. If you don't, otherwise I'm quite sure they would stop and allow your men to do all the work."

"Since you say your men could '*help*' them with the digging, I would hold off sending your servants to their property and not volunteer their services. Let the other landowners show some initiative first. My suggestion would be if the other landowners need help, let them come to you only if they start running into problems. But they will need to do some things for themselves. You should not let them take advantage of your generosity."

Tahmari thought that was only fair, then lowered her head.

"I'm so sorry. I should not have interfered with how you do business. When you hesitated, I just jumped in with my own suggestions. Please forgive me."

"Oh yes, you're correct. I agree with you. You have a great business mind, Tahmari, and your ideas are sound."

"But will your neighbors agree to that? What if they don't? Will you allow them to continue using your wells?"

"Oh, ho-ho-ho, my dear, NO!" Aheelim chuckled. "Oh yes, Tahmari, they will certainly agree. Especially if they wish to stay on good terms with me, for I am the largest landowner and without water, they would be in trouble. Right now, I have the advantage, for I am the one with the wells."

"Not long ago, my father helped them greatly when they were having a hard time during the drought. My properties are larger now than when my father had control. Once he turned the running of the family business over to me, I expanded it and have attached other properties." He continued to chuckle at this statement.

"Besides, each of them has enough servants to dig wells and do whatever else needs to be done. So let them dig their own wells. There is water to be found in the entire area for I could tell when my wells were being dug. I am certain my men will be pleased with my response."

~64~

Aheelim stood and went to the front room and surveyed his bags. He saw the packed items near the doorway and thanked her.

Lifting the bags, he turned to her and asked, "Everything is not here. Tahmari, where are your belongings?"

Tahmari lifted her eyebrows and stammered, "My-my belongings?"

He smiled at her and put one of his hands on her shoulder.

"Surely you did not think I would leave you here alone, did you? I guess I never made myself clear. I am taking you with me."

"I-I was not sure. I knew, I mean, I knew that soon you would be leaving this area, but-but…," Tahmari was stammering so much she could not finish her sentence.

"I cannot leave you here for you'll be without protection. I know after your experience in the courtyard, if those men find you again, their judgment will be worse."

"Too much has happened and you need a protector. From what you tell me, your own male relative has nothing to do with you. He would not take you in, or he would have done so before you became a prostitute. You will come with me and before we reach my home in the Valley of Tiberias, I will send messengers to inform my father and sisters of our arrival."

"We have not discussed my circumstances, but you should know that I am not a poor man and will treat you well. I have developed a certain fondness for you, but I will not touch you until we are wed."

"My father will be happy that I will wed for he keeps telling me I need a wife, and my sisters will love you. Since you are an orphan, I have no one to ask permission, but will leave the decision up to you. I asked Yahweh for a wife who would be a helpmate, and someone who would love me as much as I loved her. A woman such as you, Tahmari, and believe you are His answer."

Tahmari was aghast! It was all she could do to not have her mouth hanging open. Aheelim was speaking to her about marriage. He loved her! He loved her! Could this be happening?

Once again, her thoughts went back to Dorit's words, "If there is a man who wants to marry you and you believe he will treat you well, consider the offer. The life we live should not be the only part of our existence."

He smiled at her confusion as he continued.

"I have no family nearby since my sisters are married and no longer live with me. They are within traveling distance, but not close enough. All of them have husbands and you will soon find I have a host of nieces and nephews.

My father now lives with one of them, but he constantly reminds me it is time I married and produced an heir. He will also be happy to know that you enjoy reading the scrolls for my father has a wonderful collection."

"I never had feelings for any of the women in my area and prayed that Yahweh would find me a wife of His choosing. I desired someone who would mean more to me than just a woman with which to have sons, but a true helpmate—someone who would care for me as much as I cared for her and someone of the same mindset."

"We both believe Jesus is the Messiah and you know the value of our Jewish laws and the Commandments. An added asset is the fact that you can read, write and figure. I truly believe He found you for me."

"Even my men tell me I need to marry and I believe you would make an excellent wife and mother. You are a beautiful woman of high intelligence and I know we will fare well together. Yahweh has blessed both of us to meet—although under unusual circumstances—and has turned an impossible situation into something good. Didn't our prophet say He knows the plans He has for us? I believe this is in Yahweh's plans."

Aheelim smiled. "As the Rabbi has said, 'love is within us' and I believe it is in our relationships."

"That is," he hesitated, "if you'll have me. It was not my intention to force my plans on you and I don't want to take anything for granted. Even though I pray you won't, you have the right to turn me down."

Tahmari put her hands to the sides of her cheeks after she gave him a huge smile. She hurried back into the curtained room and quickly began gathering her belongings while crying tears of joy.

Since her items were few, and most consisted of items Aheelim had purchased for her, it took little time.

Putting Uncle Josiah's bracelet on her wrist and one of her new scarves on her head, she stopped to kneel as she gave words of praise to Yahweh.

Wiping her eyes, she finished packing the last of her clothes. She stuffed the groceries into another pack. She had saved out some of the goods so that she would have something to eat for a few days before the landlord would again rent the house. Grabbing a burlap bag, she lovingly placed Uncle Josiah's scrolls inside. Within a short time, she was ready.

After packing, she realized she had not given him an answer. Aheelim had been sitting at the table making notes on the back of dried sheepskin and rose as she entered the room.

She ran to him, put her arms around his waist and tearfully hugged him.

"I never answered your question," she stammered, "of course I'll have you. And thank you. You are the blessing Uncle Josiah always spoke of."

Aheelim smiled as he returned the hug and put her head on his shoulder. His touch reminded her of Uncle Josiah.

"You and I will be happy, Tahmari, and we will raise our future children to know the teachings of Jesus as He has taught us."

◆

As they traveled north out of town, they walked side by side in front of his horse with the mules following toward the new life they had both been given.

Tahmari could not stop smiling. She remembered the final whispered words of Yelada.

"Perhaps Yahweh will give you the desire of your heart, a good man to be your husband."

She remembered Yelada had cut her eyes at Aheelim when she said those words. How prophetic!

Aheelim suddenly stopped walking causing Tahmari and the animals to halt. He reached into one of the smaller bags and pulled out a small box. Opening it, he took out a small bracelet of tiny stones, which gleamed in the sunlight. It was richly made and fit for an Egyptian princess.

She gave a small gasp and looked into Aheelim's eyes. She had seen this bracelet before on the Oriental merchant's wagon. There was no denying that this was the very same one she had looked at and returned to the merchant.

He looked somewhat embarrassed as he held the bracelet out to her.

"I saw you once fingering some bracelets on one of the merchants' carts at the marketplace. The other day, I saw that same merchant and decided to purchase one of them. I described you and asked him what you had been selecting and then given back to him. That sly jackal knew exactly which one I was asking about and handed it to me. When I saw this one, it reminded me of you. Please accept this bracelet as my betrothal gift to you."

Tears welled up in Tahmari's eyes as she took the bracelet from his fingers. She became so emotional she could barely speak and slowly placed it on her wrist next to the bracelet Uncle Josiah gave her. It, too, was a bracelet of rich stones that only someone of wealth would wear.

Aheelim once again became embarrassed and, not knowing what to do next, bent and kissed the top of her head. Still embarrassed, he then clicked his tongue twice to start the animals moving again.

"Thank you, Aheelim. It is so beautiful," she breathed. "Thank you so very, very much."

She grabbed his hand as she reached up putting his palm against his face.

"I love it and heartily accept your betrothal gift."

As they continued on, she looked over her shoulder and saw following a short distance behind them the small dog, wagging his tail and keeping pace with the couple.

oOo

FROM THE AUTHOR

I began this book some time ago and in a discussion with my Older Adult Sunday School class, I was very surprised and impressed at how many of them (men and woman) voiced the opinion that the woman was "set-up." Why and how she was set up led to a heated discussion. One of my elderly students had me laughing, for when I explained that I was writing this story, she quipped, "She had no man who could lend a hand, and back in those days, a girl's gotta do what a girl's gotta do!"

You see, she and others felt this Jewish woman had to be desperate and at her last straw to go into this oldest profession and sympathized with her. But why was she desperate? Before the class was over, they were all on this Jewish prostitute's side, although they acknowledged the fact that she broke one of God's commandments.

Together we looked into the life of this unnamed woman, giving her a name, a past, a present and a future. Many things happened in the life of this woman before and while she was a prostitute. She had friends and enemies like any other person. What actually happened to her afterwards was not told to us in the Bible.

BIBICAL FACTS

During the time Jesus walked the earth, if there was no man for security, there was virtually little a woman could do to support herself except sell her body to feed her children and herself.

There are stories in the Bible where women did have careers of some sort, one being Lydia, a seller of dyes and purple cloth *(Acts 16:11-15, 40)*. A woman of wisdom was the character and leadership portrayed by the Judge Deborah in the Old Testament *(Judges 4)*. Naomi and Ruth had property through their dead husbands, but Boaz was a man of wealth and was able to annex Ruth and her property through a marriage of redemption *(Book of Ruth)*.

Anyone who has studied history knows there were slaves of various nations who were given to other men to be their sex partners when the master was low on funds. Female as well as male slaves were also used as prostitutes. Some masters even purchased slaves expressly to make money for themselves (early pimps?). Even today, sex trafficking of women is well known.

Many prostitutes died young due to three main problems: (i) sexually transmitted diseases; (ii) beatings by their clients (for pimps were not noted in those days); or (iii) the wives of her clients would join with the female townspeople to either stone her or run her out of town. The laws then and even now are unfair.

◆

In John 8:1-11, the woman who was "caught in adultery" had no name, although her occupation was recorded. Nothing is written as to why she became a prostitute. During this time period, there was nothing a woman could do if she had no male protector, either a husband, brother, or cousin.

In this story, both she and the man with whom she was caught have been given names and a bit of background.

My Senior Adult Bible class felt the prostitute in John 8 was "set up," but could not say why she alone was chosen to come before Jesus since Jerusalem had many such prostitutes. We went back toward other scriptures in the Bible and found most of the prostitutes who lived among the Jews were pagan.

There are many examples of prostitutes, as well as women of intelligence in the Holy Bible.

Judah had relations with his daughter-in-law Tamar, believing her to be a pagan prostitute. *(Genesis 38)*. The story details a lot about such women during the time of Jacob. In this way, Jewish men used this fact as a loophole and got around the Commandment. They felt since they were not performing fornication or adultery with a Jewish woman, using a pagan made them exempt from the Law.

Rahab was a Canaanite prostitute who was rewarded when she hid the Israelite spies prior to Jericho's destruction. She later became the wife of Salmon and begot a son named Boaz, whom we know as the kinsman-redeemer of Ruth and great-grandmother of King David *(see the genealogy of Jesus Christ in Matthew 1, especially verse 5)*.

King Solomon had to make a judgment among two arguing pagan prostitutes who brought a baby before him, each declaring the live baby to be hers and the dead baby belonging to the other. His judgment was sound when he said he would divide the baby in half. When the true mother cried out for the infant's life, he knew she was the real mother for she showed an intensity of maternal affection and not jealous possessiveness *(see I Kings 3:16-28)*.

The Book of John tells the story of the prostitute who was used by the religious leaders as they confronted Jesus concerning the Law of Moses. If they believed Jesus to be a Rabbi, that question should never have been asked; for Rabbi meant 'teacher,' and of course, a religious teacher would easily know the answers to such questions.

The prostitute brought before Jesus was Jewish and the scribes and Pharisees had to make sure she was of the Jewish faith to tempt Jesus. Why cite the Law to a woman who was not of the faith? And why bring the woman and not the man with whom she was supposedly having sex? After all, they accused her of being caught in the "very act of adultery."

"Where was the man she was caught with?" my class asked. God's Commandment states, "You must not commit adultery" *(Exodus 20:14)*. Under the Law, the penalty for adultery was severe – death for both guilty parties. If the female, whether betrothed or married, belonged to another man, and had sexual relations with another, then both would be executed. *(Deut. 22:22-24)*

The Law also sets forth that if the wife was suspected of adultery by her husband, she is required to stand trial with the priest serving as a ceremonial judge. *(Num. 5:11-31)*.

Pagan prostitutes worked on the Sabbath, Jewish holy days, etc. and would not have been brought before Jesus when the religious leaders questioned Him concerning the Law.

During class discussion, we realized the prostitute had to be Jewish to be tried by Jewish law. Hence, I used many of my seniors' comments to help write this story.

Prostitution has always been considered the "oldest profession," but back then and even now, there are many reasons why some women go into this profession.

As noted in the Book of John, the Pharisees, scribes, chief priests, and others wanted Jesus out of the way. The common people were flocking to hear him and many became followers. The people saw Jesus perform miracles and, unlike the scribes and Pharisees, taught without pomposity or strictness, explaining the love of the Father for His people, and the love of mankind to one another. Jesus expressed that He did not come to destroy the Law or the prophets; He came to fulfill the Law. *(Matt 5:17).* People came in droves to hear Him and this bothered the Jewish leaders.

According to history, the Roman government did not like the Jews to gather in multitudes for fear of a protest. There were always Jewish uprisings which commonly began with protests held by large groups. Many soldiers would be sent to quell or break up a large gathering, and there are historical writings of large groups of Jews getting together and starting riots just by following various false "messiahs".

While Jesus taught to large groups, no record is shown in scripture of Roman soldiers being sent to disperse the crowds or multitudes, whether He taught from the hills or valleys or even near the Temple.

The Roman guards, who were sent to arrest Jesus in the Garden, had no idea of what He looked like, which was why Judas Iscariot had to kiss Him to designate which of the men in the Garden of Gethsemane was the Christ *(Matthew 26:47-49).*

What is also strange is that little is mentioned about the Temple guards. These were men who guarded the

Temple and the area's synagogues and were from among the ranks of "doorkeepers." It was their job to keep order with the admittance of worshippers into the services, and the areas surrounding the buildings.

Temple guards were sent to arrest Jesus and, strangely enough, these same guards chose to join the crowds to listen to Jesus' teaching and made no arrest *(John 7:32, 44-47)*. This was a problem, for although the guards saw Him and even knew where to find Him, no arrest was ever made until He was arrested in the Garden by Roman soldiers.

The religious leaders' plots to trick Jesus continued and John 8 shows how, once again, Jesus foiled yet another attempt.

At the end of one of our lessons, a student said he had one more question to ponder:

What exactly did Jesus write in the dirt???

My response to that question: "Class, when we get to heaven, perhaps we would then have the opportunity ask Him."

~oOo~

LSW

CHARACTERS IN THIS STORY

Tahmari – Jewish prostitute
Aheelim – Man caught in situation with Tahmari
Abner – Livery and stable owner; Goshen's boss
Arbor – Eunuch - servant of Dorit
Batlan – Yelada's husband
Burlaht – Prostitute who died in childbirth
Dorit – Older prostitute and mentor
Elema – Goshen's baby sister
Eliah – Town official, friend to Teheran
Garner – Prostitute and friend of Tahmari
Goshen – Jepthun, a runaway slave
Halah – Josiah's wife
Jaffal and Jakri – Talkative twins
Josiah – Tahmari's uncle
Kiri – Prostitute and friend of Tahmari
Luchi – Prostitute and friend of Tahmari
Marka – Cousin Shallum's wife
Meka – Josiah's housekeeper
Mogdi – Tahmari's childhood friend
Najur – Arbor's friend and eunuch
Pashur – Abner's nephew and fellow worker
Pooka Family – Foreign merchant traders
Samtil – Town official
Shallum – Estranged Cousin of Josiah
Suri – Arbor's older sister
Teheran – Town official
Tirshah – Goshen's female friend; Abner's niece
Turza – Kiri's friend
Yelada – Young woman who was raped

* Scriptures are paraphrased from the New King James Version.

Printed in the United States
By Bookmasters

Printed in the United States
By Bookmasters